4 Feb 2000

Jim & Nancy

THE GIFT OF THE HOLY CROSS

enjoy the novel
and know about God-life

regards,

LINO LEITÃO

THE GIFT OF THE HOLY CROSS

PEEPAL TREE

First published in Great Britain in 1999
Peepal Tree Press Ltd.
17 King's Avenue
Leeds LS6 1QS
England

ISBN 1 900715 15 7

ACKNOWLEDGEMENTS

I thank the Canada Council for awarding me a grant to write this novel.

I thank Dr. John Hobgood and Professor Peter Nazareth for reading the original manuscript of this book and offering me encouragement and suggestions. I am grateful to Rosemary Leaver who did the final proofreading of the manuscript. Besides I must thank Peter Leaver and Fritz Lewertoff, the connoisseurs of good beer and fiction, who read the original manuscript and saw the possibility of its publication.

for my wife
Olga Mecrina

PREFACE

This story is set in Goa, a former Portuguese colony in India. It tries to analyse the colonial system and the mores bestowed upon the colonised populace of Goa. As the story moves along, it comes to present-day Goa, a Goa free of Portuguese colonialism.

Though there are historical incidents and personalities in *The Gift of the Holy Cross*, it is not a historical novel. Nor is it the historical story of the two villages, Carmona and Cavelossim. It is a fictional story. Historical incidents are made to fit into the novel's narrative, and the characters in it are from the author's imagination. No reference to any persons living or dead is intended.

The writing of the novel was completed in 1983.

Lino Leitão
Dorval, January 1997

BOOK I

CHAPTER I

Never had rain been so late. The villagers scanned the sky. Not a cloud. The sun blazed with fury. Rivers, streams, ponds and wells had dried up. Not knowing what else to do, the people gathered at dawn and dug deeper and deeper into the beds of water sources. After much effort, a trickle of water would emerge, hardly enough to fill a pitcher.

The paddy fields were bowls of dust. The coconut palms had dropped their fronds and were without a nut. The banyan trees, whose green foliage once provided shade, had shed their leaves. Animals got sick and died. Cholera, typhoid and a host of other diseases were rampant. No Goan alive remembered such a severe drought, not even Jozin-Bab, the centenarian of the village of Cavelossim. The torment brought by thirst and hunger to men and animals made him angry with God. God was cruel. Jozin-Bab could no longer tolerate the ungodliness of God. In a fit of anger, he took out the miraculous statuette of Saint Anthony from his *oratorio* and spoke to it in raspy, intimidating tones, "Whenever there was drought, I prayed to you and rain came. Our lands gave bountiful yields. But today, all of Goa is praying and your heart isn't moved. Cruel, that's what you are! You have all the comfort of the oratorio. Now, I'm going to throw you down the village well. You'll see for yourself how dry it is. Then perhaps you'll know our anguish. And then, perhaps, you'll make it rain."

Jozin-Bab walked with his staff in one hand and the statuette in the other to the well. He looked at the statuette for the last time, then dropped it down the shaft. "That's where you'll stay if doesn't rain soon," he shouted.

The chaplain was furious and said it was a sacrilege. But the villagers forgave Jozin-Bab thinking he'd gone senile, and many hoped that the statuette would get lonely at the bottom of the well and bring rain.

No rain came.

The villagers did not stop praying. But God was deaf to their prayers. God was deaf to the cries of the beasts. They took the statue of Saint Anthony in procession. They dragged themselves on their knees, begging him,

> Saint Anthony,
> Saint Anthony,
> Make it rain!
> Make it rain!
> Have pity on us.

Their land was as dry as ever.

Inside the chapel of the Holy Cross of Cavelossim, the faithful gathered one sultry evening. Men and women were on their knees, hands folded in prayer, pleading eyes fixed on the altar. Even the flames of the lit tapers seemed palely sad. The whole congregation reverently chanted the invocation to the Holy Cross:

> Holy Cross,
> Strength of Christians,
> Helper of Christians,
> Save us all,
> Save us,
> Forever,
> Holy Cross...

They came to the end of their chanting. Silence descended on the shadowed chapel. From the altars the saints looked down on them. Into the elevated pulpit came the preacher. The women squatted on the floor, though not the wives and daughters of the village notables, who sat on the benches at the back, behind them. Also sitting were the male notables. The rest of the males stood.

In spite of the stifling heat, none of the women unfolded their tiny fans to stir a breath of air. The preacher looked at the haggard congregation. They craned their necks and cocked their ears to listen. He was the man of God and bound to know their sins. He would admonish them to repent. And when they had done their penance, perhaps God would make it rain on their lands.

The preacher was a young man, in his mid-thirties. He was tall, handsome, well-fed and much fairer than the villagers. The faithful knew that he had studied in Rome, which in those days was next to

Heaven. He ranked higher than their chaplain; in fact, nearer to God than anybody they knew.

The taper flames barely moved. The whole universe seemed at a standstill. The congregation waited anxiously. At long last, the preacher made the sign of the cross. Like a thunderbolt came his voice. The sunken eyes of the congregation widened and their jaws fell as the preacher began bellowing in Latin. God above did not know the language of these unworthy mortals. His voice rose and fell like the waves of a turbulent sea, dashing into the souls of the congregation. There were tears in their eyes and remorse in their hearts. He continued in Konkani: "When you wallow in sin, do you ever think that there is God above?" His eyes flared and he pounded his fist on the pulpit.

His listeners, like cows driven to a slaughterhouse, felt that the hand of God would get them now.

"Your sins surpass all understanding. Why shouldn't God punish you?" He looked down over them. "You will writhe and die of thirst and hunger. Now is the time to remember all the sins that you have committed. Remember them now and repent."

The congregation fell to their knees, folding their hands in prayer and remembrance. The preacher stood in the pulpit facing the Eucharist like the rest. But he was relaxed. He wiped his forehead with a clean handkerchief and drank a glass of water.

A peasant woman, Patrocin, remembered that she had taken a fallen palm leaf from her landlord's land. Tears came to her eyes and she let out a loud sigh. The preacher looked down at her reproachfully. Bosteão Menin, the village launderer, sobbed, "Never again, never again, my Lord." He had muttered curses against his landlord. At that time he had thanked his stars that the landlord hadn't heard him, but now God was punishing not only him but everybody. All of them remembered their sins. They were appalled at the blackness in their hearts. They vowed to tread the path of God; to live in subjugation to their superiors on earth.

The preacher resumed his sermon.

"I ask of you women," he roared, "Who among you will give a son to the Holy Cross? Who? Who?"

Silence hung like a sword. The saints on the altars waited for an answer. The preacher's eyes went from woman to woman. His voice swelled, "Who will give a son, a son to be nailed to the Holy Cross? Who? Who?"

He paused, making them hear the silence, and pointing his finger to each of them, he shouted, "None of you! None of you!"

They cast their heads down.

"Your sufferings are nothing. Can they be compared to the agonies of Christ on the Cross? Dare you make such a comparison? Don't you remember that Jesus' throat was parched with thirst? He cried for water. Was he given any water? Was he?"

He surveyed his flock. He knew what they were thinking.

"A sponge wetted in vinegar was pushed into Jesus' parched mouth. Your sufferings are nothing, nothing at all. Each of you ask this question: Why is God inflicting these sufferings on me?"

He awaited their answer. The taper flames and the saints on the altar waited too. Some lips moved. The preacher wiped his forehead and drank another glass of water.

"God has inflicted pain on you because you're sinners. How can you make up with God? How?" He gazed at the congregation. Their eyes said they would do anything to make up with God.

"God wants your sons," he declared. "Yes, your sons. Give your sons to the Holy Cross. Give."

Most of the congregation was baffled. They understood his rhetoric. He was asking their sons to become priests. But how? The lower castes were barred from becoming priests.

"You must count your blessings as Catholics," he intoned. "There are millions in this world who haven't seen the Light. God wants your sons to propagate His Kingdom. God wants you to suffer for his sake as Christ did for yours. Who among you will make a solemn promise to give a son to the Holy Cross."

He stared at the women like a hawk. Then his eyes met those of a woman which gleamed back at him. A stir went through him.

"Give your son to the Holy Cross and your sufferings will turn into joy," he said as if directly addressing her. "When your throat is dry, God will never give you a drink of vinegar. God is infinitely merciful. Will you not give your son to the Holy Cross?"

The woman's lips quivered and her eyes brimmed with tears. Inaudibly, she vowed, "God give me a son and I'll present him as a gift to the Holy Cross."

The woman was *Dona* Rosa Jaques, the wife for more than fifteen years of *senhor* Brito Maximiano Jaques, during which she had not been blessed with a child. As a barren woman, though of higher caste, she had been without respect in the village. Though lower-caste people called her *Ocobae*, in any squabble she had with them, they never hesitated to throw her barrenness in her face. She had never ceased to pray with all humility for a child.

Merciful God had at last taken pity on her, and though Rosa was in her ninth month, she was glad that she had come to the chapel that evening. The sermon had moved her and she had made a solemn vow to the Holy Cross. She was sure that God would give her a son now.

The service was at last over and the faithful began to leave the chapel. As Rosa moved cumbrously towards the door, she felt warm liquid oozing down her thighs. She stopped and squatted on the floor.

"What's wrong *Ocobae*?" asked Ermelin, her neighbour.

"My time's come, I think."

"Of course, it has," agreed Carolin, an old woman, who pushed aside the crowd around Rosa. "You shouldn't have come."

Rosa smiled faintly.

Then, on Carolin's instructions, two hefty villagers lifted Rosa to her feet and helped her to walk home, her waters streaming down her legs. She did not live far from the chapel and they were able to get her to her room and lay her on her mat.

"Has anyone gone for Oji-mai Concentin?" Carolin asked.

"Alxin has gone on Pancras' bike," said Ermelin. "But who is warming up the water? Before Ocobae delivers, shouldn't she be given a wash?"

"We'd better give her a shave and enema too, before Oji-mai arrives," said Carolin.

Someone was sent to look for a razor. There was hardly any water in Rosa's house and Carolin sent off Alba, a thirteen-year-old girl who was hanging about the house, to find some water.

"From where?"

"From anywhere."

Alba looked at Carolin, puzzled.

"Go from house to house and tell them that *Ocobae* is about to deliver. They will give the drop of water they have."

Alba ran off on her errand. She collected enough water to fill the *ban* and put it to boil on the hearth in the yard.

By now, Oji-mai Concentin could be seen hurrying towards the house. She was in her forties, thin as a rail but wiry and neat. Though the air was still, her hasty tiptoe walk gave the impression that she was being carried along by the wind. Nearing the house, she girded her *capor* and called out, "Is everything set?"

The women nodded.

Rosa had been shaved, washed and given an enema. In the delivery room, there was a basin of hot steaming water, a pile of clean rags, pads of cotton, some pins, a pair of scissors and a bottle of *feni*. On the wall, there was a panel of Our Lady of Bom Parto and before it, a small votive lamp.

Concentin pressed Rosa's bulging stomach. She nodded in approval of her diagnosis. The other women eyed her anxiously.

"The baby is due at any time," she declared. "Can someone get me holy water?"

"Where do you keep your holy water, Ocobae?" Ermelin asked.

"In the cupboard of the *dispens*. It's in a white bottle."

Concentin poured the holy water on Rosa's stomach. She made the sign of the cross and offered three Hail Marys to Our Lady of Bom Parto for Rosa's safe delivery. The other women prayed too.

By now Rosa was having contractions every five minutes. She looked up anxiously and Concentin, who had been delivering babies for years, smiled reassuringly and said, "It'll be over soon, Ocobae. You'll be a mother before you know it."

The pains were constant now and Rosa screamed in agony. Ermelin and the other women comforted her, wiping the sweat from her forehead.

"Push hard! Push hard!" Oji-mai Concentin shouted. "Unless you push hard, the baby won't come out. Push! Push!"

Rosa was doing her best.

"You'll forget these pains, Ocobae," she said, "when you have a fine boy in your arms."

But some time later, the baby still hadn't arrived. Concentin was concerned. The baby should have been crowning by now. She put her hands into Rosa's vagina and urged her to push harder. Suddenly, a flash of lightning lit up the shadowy room, dazzling her eyes. "Jesus!" cried Concentin, and at that instant, in a flood of blood and birth liquids, her deft hands brought forth the baby. She looked at the newborn's face. It was made radiant by a second flash of lightning. Was she holding a human or divine child? There was a deep rumble in the sky – the voice of God above. The room should have smelled of steamy hot water and human blood, but when Concentin inhaled, what she smelled was an exquisite fragrance. This would be a blessed baby. Then Concentin heard thick drops of rain pattering on the roof. Now the earth would be dressed in green and become fruitful again.

From outside came joyous cries, "Rain! Rain! Rain!"

In Concentin's ears it sounded like, "He's born! He's born!"

"A boy?" Rosa asked feebly.

"Yes."

On Rosa's face, in spite of her exhaustion, there was a glow of ecstasy. Concentin felt sure that Rosa knew the secret behind her son's birth.

All the mess from the delivery room was cleared. Into a hollow tile glowing with charcoal stones, a handful of frankincense was put and its fragrance filled the whole house. In the oratorio candles were lit. Rosa was now dressed and laid on the bed, looking spent and flat. The child was laid next to her – clean and chubby, swaddled in white.

Alxin hurried to Bascor's shop and brought three packs of firecrackers and set these off on Rosa's balcony, one after the other. Those who heard them knew that Rosa had delivered a son; for a girl, only two packs of firecrackers were fired.

It was getting late. Concentin wanted to go home. The customary payment was made to her: a bottle of feni, two unhusked coconuts, a measure of rice and a couple of rupees.

"Concentin," said Rosa. "Thank you for bringing my son safely into this world."

Then Rosa's brother Lorenço came with a goblet and bottle of feni. He poured out some and offered it to Concentin.

"I've delivered many babies, *Bab*," she said taking a sip from her drink, "but I tell you, this isn't an ordinary child. Did you notice anything, Ocobae?"

"Notice what, Concentin?" asked Rosa.

"That the baby didn't cry as he came into this world."

"He didn't?" asked Lorenço, surprised.

"No, Bab," she said, "I saw a smile on his face. It was as bright as that lightning."

Rosa smiled. In her heart she knew that her son was the gift of God and that the Holy Cross would claim him in due course.

"Look at him," said Concentin pointing to the newborn, "he seems to understand already what we are talking about. I tell you Ocobae, this son of yours is blessed. The very instant of his coming into this world, rain came down on our parched earth. What do say to that, Ocobae?"

A wave of ecstasy went through Rosa.

"Your son brought rain," said Concentin. "Do you know what it means? Something within me says that your son is the harbinger of joy to us all."

Concentin looked at the newborn. "I drink to your health, my little one."

"Take another one, Concentin," said Rosa, and Concentin did not refuse.

"Well, I must go now," she said. "It's raining outside. Is there a *kondo*, Ocobae?"

Someone brought her a kondo and Carolin gave her a torch of palm leaves to light her way home.

"Take care Ocobae; take care of the little one," she said as she departed.

CHAPTER II

It was a dark night as Oji-mai Concentin hurried home. Her torch of palm leaves was already dead. But now and then the sky was rent by a flash of lightning and Concentin knew the pathways of the village like the palms of her hands.

She had never felt so content. She could hear the earth slaking its thirst; she could almost see the trees and bushes as they quenched their thirst, too. The earth smelt sweet.

As she hurried home, she saw kerosene lamps flickering in the villagers' houses. These were votive lights to thank God for the rain. Did the people know that it was Ocobae Rosa's infant who had saved them from thirst and hunger? Did they know who had brought the infant into the world? She looked upwards. A thick blanket of monsoon clouds covered the sky. Yet there was a star, a bright solitary star, far off in the sky. Tears rushed to her eyes.

"Then it is true, God," she whispered, "that Ocobae's son is..." Like the star in the inky blackness of the clouds, the child from Rosa's womb would grow into a man who would shine in the darkness of mankind. But would mankind see this light? To them the star might be too far off. Her thoughts were disturbed by shouts coming from the village. She recognised the voice of her neighbour, Ubald-Bab.

"Marialin! Marialin!" he was shouting. "The roof is leaking here. It's become a lake! Are you deaf, Marialin? Quick! Quick! Get a can here, you trollop!"

"This Ubald-Bab is crazy. Can't he get the can himself?" Concentin said angrily to herself.

Arriving home, she left the kondo on the balcony to drip and went in. She put the feni, the rice and the coconuts in a corner of the room. She lit the kerosene lamp and sat on her *bakin*.

Concentin lived alone in a small mud house on her landlord's land. Her only daughter, Piedade, was married five villages away. She hated to be alone in the house and would often go and stay with her daughter, but tonight she wanted no company. She wasn't hungry, but wanted only a cup of hot tea. Luckily she had a basketful of dry leaves in the kitchen, more than enough to boil the tea pot. She put the steaming hot tea into the mug added two spoons of sugar, stirred it and had a sip.

The frail flame of the kerosene lamp flickered in the breeze. She sipped her tea, meditating. The more she thought about it, the more convinced she was that Rosa's son was the gift of God. The aroma at his birth still lingered in her nostrils. Then she looked at her hands. Skinny and wrinkled as they were, from how many wombs had they brought forth life? She said softly, "You have blessed these hands of mine. I thank you, God."

A gust of wind came through a crack in the window and blew out the lamp. Still deep in thought, Concentin scarcely noticed that she had been plunged into darkness. Then, as tiredness numbed her brain, she fell asleep, still leaning against the wall, her legs outstretched on the floor.

At first smiles flickered on her face, but then she began to move restlessly and moan in distress. She was dreaming. She saw giant tongues of fire in infinite space. Red hot flames burning bright. Into it many people were cast, screaming. She saw their hands raised in a futile attempt to keep away from the inferno, terror on their faces. She looked closely and was surprised to see Julia, an elderly spinster who had died a year ago, among the crowd. How could she be there? To the villagers, she had been a saint.

She was still in her dream, looking and looking, but she didn't know for whom. Then she realised it was her parents and husband she sought. Could they be here too? To her relief she couldn't see them. They'd had the last sacraments just before they died. Shouldn't that absolve their sins? Then she heard music coming from a trumpet. This wasn't Hell but Purgatory. Dread seized her that her parents and her husband weren't there because they might be in Hell.

"Almighty God," she prayed, "please save them."

She now saw a cherub playing on the trumpet approaching the flames. The music soothed the suffering multitude, but when the cherub was a few paces from the fire, she heard, "Take me out from here! Take me to Heaven!" There was pain on the cherub's face; he couldn't take all of them with him. He picked up only those who had finished their penance and floated away with them. The others were left to their torment.

Concentin awoke in cold panic. It was all too clear that the dead couldn't trust their relatives on earth. The living soon forgot them. She would put away some money with the village chaplain to say masses for her soul when she died. If she was condemned to Purgatory, she didn't want to stay there long.

Suddenly, it struck her that the cherub was Rosa's son. He had the same lustre and features. God was revealing the future to her. But there was something puzzlingly familiar about those scenes in her dream. Yes, she remembered now that there was a painting of Purgatory by Crispin, the village artist, on the wall of the cemetery. It was under the heading, "MAN, LOOK BEFORE YOU COMMIT SIN." But how did he know how to paint Purgatory? God must have shown it to him, too. The picture of Hell was there as well, with a horde of black devils, with horns and tails. That picture always made her shudder.

She thought about other slogans on the cemetery wall. Some of them were in Portuguese. One said, "IRMÃOS! FUI O QUE VOS SOIS; VOS SEREIS QUE EU SOU." This was under a drawing of a human skeleton. *Brothers! I was what you are; you will be what I am.* Another said, A MORTE IGUALA A COROA COM ENXADA E A NOBREZA COM VILEZA. *Death levels the crown with the spade and the noble with the peasant.* There was truth in that. In death, the labourer dripping with sweat and the mighty and pompous noble both turn into dust. However, the slogan which meant most to her said, in Konkani, VOHODD SUC MUNXAC BOREM MORON – *The greatest happiness for any human is a death free from sin.* She wanted to go neither to Purgatory nor to Hell, but straight to Heaven, and that reminded her of the slogan that said, JIVIT TOXEM MORON – *The way you live is the way you will die.* What kind of life had she lived? Who would come to claim her soul? Angels or Devils? The thought of Hell sent shivers up and down her spine. In the bloom of her youth, she had had many temptations, and as she remembered them now, anguish welled up. She had been tall and slim, and her breasts, like papaya in her blouse, were the cause of stares and sometimes outright harassment from the village notables.

Once she had succumbed. Her mother had sent her to senhor Dias' house to ask for money he owed her. Senhor Dias, the respected *Regedor* of the village, wasn't in, but his son, Fernando, was there. He was a tall, handsome youth, not yet twenty. Taking advantage of his parents' absence, he embraced her and though she exhibited a graceful reluctance, she had been excited by his caresses. He had opened her blouse and held her breasts in his hands, fondling and admiring them. He had taken one breast into his mouth, sending tremors through her body. Then he had stripped her naked, as if he were skinning a rabbit. There was no reluctance on her part any more; he had shed his clothes, too, and then, on his parents' bed, the oligarch's son had taken her to heaven. But when she came down to earth, shame and guilt gnawed at her like twin rats. In the end, she had gone to confession, but not to her chaplain. No one could trust him not to make references to their confessions in his Sunday homilies and then the whole village knew about them.

She had gone on foot to Old Goa. All the way, she had mouthed the decades of the rosary that she might be saved from the fires of everlasting Hell. Arriving at Bom Jesus Basilica, she had fallen on her knees before the tomb of St. Francis Xavier and asked him to have pity on her. He had converted her pagan ancestors to Christianity; wouldn't he save her from the torments of Hell? With tears in her eyes and remorse in her heart, she had confessed her sins. The confessor had lectured her harshly about the sins of the flesh and given her a very heavy penance. This she had done without wavering. Recollecting this, she felt calmer and went back to sleep.

But when she dreamt again, she saw herself being consumed by hellish flames, surrounded by horny devils with big tails, dancing. She was calling, "Take me out! Take me out from here!"

"You of little faith," she heard someone whisper.

Looking around she saw the cherub again. He said, "You brought me out from my mother's womb, Oji-mai. I'll take you out of this fire pit." Though she was consoled, she dreamt again and saw a huge cross; it was empty and looked as if it was waiting for its human burden.

She woke, panting and sweating, disturbed by the noise of exploding firecrackers. She heard someone calling out, "Marialin, get up! Get up, Marialin! The fox is taking our piglet."

Another firecracker exploded.

It was Ubald-Bab. Was he in Hell?

Again, she heard him shouting, "Marialin, *pezeco uzo gali.* It's dawn already."

Concentin was now fully awake. She felt stiff and wondered how she came to be on the floor, propped against the wall. Outside the birds were singing and Ermelin's rooster was loudly announcing the dawn. She heard Tar Menin's buffaloes lowing. She hauled herself painfully to her feet. The chapel bell would soon be tolling for the morning angelus. She looked out through the door. The village was awake. The rain had stopped and the sun was bright again.

CHAPTER III

It was a beautiful Sunday. The people of Cavelossim had smiles on their faces as they answered the call of the chapel bell. Dressed in their church clothes they hurried down the narrow twisting paths, the married women in *oli*, and some wearing *chinels* on their feet; the spinsters in long frocks and mantillas over their heads; those who could read carrying a prayer book in one hand and rosary beads in the other. The village notables came in white trousers and white turtleneck coats, sandals on their feet, most carrying a cane. The poor men from the lower castes wore *cabai*, like Roman tunics, and walked barefoot. The Holy Cross had heard their prayers, but Oji-mai Concentin felt she alone knew who had caused the rain.

As the villagers walked to the chapel, they talked enthusiastically about the cultivation of the paddy fields.

"What manure are you going to use this year, senhor Tolentinho?" asked Dr. Maurice-Bab, one of the notables.

"I really don't know, Dr. Maurice," answered Tolentinho, swinging his cane, "but I think, I'll stick to fish fertilizer. Last year it gave good results; and you, Doctor?"

"I'll heed Mud Bosteão's advice."

"What does he want you to use?"

"Pig and cow dung. Mud Bosteão says a paddy field shouldn't be given the same fertilizer year after year. Change gives good results. I think he's right."

Dr. Maurice noticed Concentin hurrying behind them. He called out to her and she, startled, stopped in her tracks. "Yes, Dr.-Bab?" she said humbly.

"You look happy this morning. What happened?"

A smile bloomed on her face. "Don't you know, Dr-Bab?"

"Know what, Concentin?"

"Ocobae Rosa delivered, Dr.-Bab. No complications; hence there wasn't need to call you."

"A boy or a girl?" Tolentinho asked.

"A boy, Tolentinho-Bab."

"Good," said Dr. Maurice, "and that's why you're happy?"

Concentin told him about the birth of Rosa's son, the lightning and the rain.

"Rosa has a beautiful baby then?" asked Dr. Maurice.

"When he came in my hands, he was pure white, as if he wasn't from this wretched world."

"Such a beauty? Hm."

"You don't understand, Dr.-Bab," Concentin said. "When I held the baby in my hands, his eyes were so bright."

She wanted to tell them all about her dream. These were village notables, people full of wisdom and knowledge, who knew how to read and write. They would know the significance of her dream. However, she would not tell them about it. Certain things must be kept secret, even from notables.

The last bell for the service rang. Concentin, excusing herself, hurried to the chapel. This was not the day to be late.

Inside, the chapel was packed. A mass was to be sung in celebration of their joy. Vicente-*mestri*, the parish teacher, looking important in his bifocals, was playing the harmonium in the chapel loft. The village choir — Asselmo Rosa, Evaristo Rodrigues, Menino Costa and others — were raising their voices to Heaven.

Today, the tapers on the altars smiled affectionately. Throughout the service Oji-mai Concentin was in a trance. Was she in Heaven? Or was she still in her dream? She had to be shaken by Modo-mai Majakin, the village washerwoman, who asked her, "Aren't you coming home, Concentin? Mass is over. You look as if you're in Heaven."

"I am. Don't you know?"

"Know what?"

"Ocobae Rosa delivered a boy."

"Is that so!" said Modo-mai. "My grandchild said he heard firecrackers exploding. But, you know, it was raining..."

As they walked home, Concentin told her about the birth of Rosa's son, Modo-mai interrupting her here and there.

Though Modo-mai was old now, she still did the laundry for the Jaques household and a few other families. She had a deep affection for Maximiano Brito Jaques; she called him, *mujea puta* – my son – because when his mother had died in childbirth, it was she who, having given birth to her own son a few days earlier, had given her breasts to Maximiano, nursing him with tender love and care. As an adult, Maximiano had never failed to show her his gratitude, often giving her gifts of tobacco and sometimes money.

She had been sorry for him all those years when Rosa couldn't conceive. She had made vows to the saints, had lit candles and gone on her knees to them. Like all Goans she felt that every household needed a son to light the lamp in the house, to continue the lineage and maintain the family cult. Otherwise, what is the existence of man? So Modo-mai was overjoyed when she learnt of Rosa's pregnancy, though she was hurt that she hadn't been there at the delivery.

"Concentin," she said, "how wonderful is God that he blessed the womb of Ocobae with a son! And you say the child is divine? That at his coming the rain came? Concentin, I'm hurrying to Ocobae's house. I want to see my *morgado*."

At Rosa's house, Modo-mai poured out her apologies for missing the birth, asked anxiously after Rosa's health and demanded to know what help she was getting in the house.

"It's all right," Rosa told her. "At present, one-eyed Mariano's daughter, Joanit, is helping out."

"That's good. But I'll come every evening and massage you with coconut oil. That will bring your strength back. Do you have enough milk in your breasts?"

"My breasts are bursting with milk."

"Good, good. But you know, if you want to keep your supply up, you must eat coconut kernel every day."

When the baby had finished feeding, Modo-mai begged Rosa to let her hold him. She took him in her wrinkled hands and patted his back, remembering Maximiano.

"He looks exactly like his father," she said.

Rosa smiled.

"But Ocobae, did you protect my morgado against *dist*? You haven't yet put a black dot on the little one's face."

"But..."

"Don't want to hear your excuses," she said, and giving the baby back to Rosa, she hurried off to the pantry, returning with a couple of dry red chillies, a few grains of husked rice and some salt.

As Rosa held the child in her arms, Modo-mai traced the sign of the cross with one of the chillies on his forehead, lips, chest and on many other parts of his body. Taking salt and rice in her hand she repeated the same process, and then, taking all these ingredients together in her hands, she circled them above the baby's head three times, saying the Credo and commanding evil spirits to depart. To complete the ritual, she put the ingredients into a hollow tile

containing burning charcoal and soon the place was filled with a
pungent smell and the noise of the exploding salt. Modo-mai spat into
it three times, "*Hak tu! Hak tu! Hak tu!*" Finally, she walked out of
the house with the tile and dropped it into a gutter, far enough away.

"You know, Ocobae," Modo-mai advised, coming back, "you
should do this often. I used to do this to your husband when he was
a baby and even when he was grown up. Call Rosalin Mauxi now and
then. She's an expert in such things."

"I will."

"Now, let me put the black dot on my morgado's cheek."

From the kitchen she collected a pinch of soot and mixed it with
a few drops of coconut oil. With the little finger of her right hand she
put a black dot on the baby's left cheek.

"Now," she said, "all eyes will be drawn to this spot, and no
jealous eyes will notice how comely he is."

Modo-mai drank a goblet of feni that Rosa had offered. Before
leaving, she said, "Hope God's angel writes a good destiny for my
little one when he visits him on the sixth night."

Rosa suddenly felt sad and she sighed.

CHAPTER IV

The village wells now were filled almost to the brim. Once again, the young women, chattering and giggling, earthen pots on their left hips and copper pots and ropes in their right hands, made their regular trips to the well. This was a centre for news; and here, Sofi, nicknamed *O Heraldo* by her friends, after a Goan daily newspaper, was announcing: "Have you seen Rosa-Bae's infant? He's the very incarnation of an angel. And do you know?"

"Know what, *O Heraldo*?"

"It's he who brought us rain."

The news spread and villagers from all around came to visit Rosa's son. When they saw him, they told her, "Ocobae, your son brought us rain and the promise of food. He's no doubt a heavenly offspring. May he grow into a man to save us all."

Such exaltations reminded Rosa of the vow that she had made to the Holy Cross. Wrapped in silence, she would brood about her son. What was in store for him?

"Don't cast admiring glances at my morgado," Modo-mai warned the visitors, when she was around. "You might cast dist on him. And then..."

One day, the village centenarian, Jozin-Bab, staff in hand, came to see the infant.

"Jozin-Bab," Rosa said respectfully, giving him a chair.

"Rosa," he said, "is it true what they say about your son?"

Rosa's eyes clouded with tears. She kept quiet.

"Let me see your son."

Rosa brought him the child and Jozin-Bab stood up and held the child, gazing down into his eyes. At that very moment, the chapel bell rang for the noon angelus. A mystical look came upon Jozin-Bab's face and, with passion, he said the angelus.

"I see my own resurrection through your infant," he told Rosa when he had finished the prayer.

The infant reached up and touched Jozin-Bab's wrinkled face. Tears came in his eyes and with a trembling voice, he said, "Now, I know why my Saint Anthony didn't bring rain. It was left to your son to perform this miracle. Your son's coming showered the thirsty soil with water and made our pastures green. You know, what that means, don't you?" He paused. "In my youth I heard that the white crows came and ate the black crows. But in the future the black crows would eat the black crows."

Rosa listened attentively, though she couldn't understand the old man's riddles. He gave back the child and sat down. Rosa went to the pantry to bring him a goblet of *feni*. Before sipping the drink, he spoke again. "Your son will be a good farmer who keeps his farm free from weeds. He will sow a new strain of seeds bred to resist disease and pests."

Tears trickled down Rosa's cheek as she listened. "Don't waste your tears now, Rosa," said Jozin-Bab, gulping down his drink, "like Dud-Sagor Falls your tears will flow. Save them for later."

"But, Jozin-Bab why do you talk like that?"

"I don't know, Rosa, but I know what I say will come to pass."

She clutched the baby closer to her bosom.

"When the seed is sown," he continued, taking a sip from the second drink she offered him, "it bursts and brings forth a plant and the plant yields identical seeds. Your son is the seed of mankind, but I fear he is a seed that has been planted among thorny bushes. He will struggle to come up..." Jozin-Bab looked as if he had more to say, but he stopped when he saw the distress on Rosa's face. "Rosa," he said, "you know, it is through suffering that one knows real happiness."

She looked at him uncertainly, wishing more and more that she could be like any other mother in the village, her child ordinary and unremarked.

CHAPTER V

When Rosa's son was eight days old he was baptised according to custom. Maximiano had wanted important notables as godparents for their son, but though Rosa knew the advantages of such relationships, she was against it. Her son was the gift of the Holy Cross and if she chose godparents from the lower castes, it would be a sign of her humility. She was so convinced of this that, in the end, Maximiano left the matter to her.

There were many God-fearing people in the village, but for godfather Rosa chose Hut João, their *mundcar*. He was a young unmarried man, a labourer on their paddy fields, who was poor and lived with his parents in a palm-thatched hut. He was meekly obedient to the church and the notables, a man who knew his place. Rosa often summoned him to chop wood and do odd jobs for her, and even if he was tired, he never let her down.

He was hewing wood in her yard one hot afternoon, sweat beads glistening on his dark, naked body, when she came to speak to him.

"João," she said in a motherly voice.

"Yes, Ocobae."

"I want you to be the godfather of my child."

"Me!"

"Yes, you João; that's what I want."

Who was he to go against her wish? It was truly an honour for such a humble person as he.

For godmother, Rosa chose Neunita Figueredo. She was the daughter of a former Regedor, a choice that would please her husband. Neunita was a devout woman who went to chapel daily to receive the Eucharist, the annunciator of the rosary at the chapel, the leader of the Legion of Mary and always the first to arrive at the bedside of a dying person to invoke help for them. Her dresses were long and all-covering, her breasts flattened with yards of linen, to avoid tempting the village men. Rumour had it that she had been hurt in a love affair and had gone away to become a nun and that she had taken a casket of soil from the village cemetery to be thrown into her grave. Though she had come back to the village, she had kept her vow to remain *beata* and devote her life to God. Neunita willingly agreed to be the godmother of Rosa's child.

Rosa planned the customary *ladainha* for the christening. Because she knew she wouldn't be pregnant again, she wanted the memory of this occasion to last. The whole village was invited. Mazancit, the village cook, was ordered to prepare *soupa verde* and *arroz refugado*; and Inas, the toddy tapper and distiller, was given an order to supply the best feni *codso*; *branco* was bought for the children and beer and *maceira* for the notables.

At 11 a.m. on that great day, firecrackers burst on the chapel's patio and the bell chimed as Rosa's son was baptised. He was named Mario Santana Arsenio de Santa Almas Jaques. He was named Mario after Maximiano's late father. Rosa couldn't leave out her own dead father's name, if she did, he would be annoyed, wherever he was, and hence the second name for her son – Santana. Now both grandfathers would rejoice and come to her son's aid if he were in trouble. She also named him Arsenio because that was the name of her only brother-in-law, who had died young; so his name had to be perpetuated too. Wanting total protection for her son, Rosa left nothing to chance, so he was called Santa Almas, Holy Souls. Now the whole legion of saintly souls would bless, guide and protect him throughout his earthly life. Mario, though, was the name that he would be called by.

After the service, Neunita carried the infant in his long white gown, accompanied by Hut João and the baptismal party to Rosa's house. Hut João, wearing his best clothes, a coat over his creased shirt and a pair of patched trousers to cover his usually bare legs, walked solemnly, fingering his rosary and moving his lips.

Before crossing the threshold of the house, Rosa circled a container of sweetly burning frankincense above her son's head. Firecrackers were set off on her veranda, and the village knew that her son had been christened.

Mario was put in his cot, tired by the ceremony. The godparents and the guests knelt before the oratorio, lit with candles, praying that Mario grow into a good Catholic, an example to the whole village. Long after the others had finished praying, Rosa was still on her knees, tears in her eyes.

In the evening, guests streamed to Rosa's house for ladainha. Some who had arrived early complained, "It's already nine. When are they going to start?"

"They're waiting for the bigwigs," someone said.

"Bigwigs won't come unless we start. They come only to eat and drink, don't they?"

They all laughed.

The chaplain assured them that there were now enough singers present. Rosa agreed and signalled Ubald-Bab, the village fiddler, to tune up his violin. As he waxed his bow, the vocalists, one by one, gave samples of their tunes.

"Will this one do?" asked one.

"It's too complicated," others said.

"This one?"

"That's too common. It doesn't fit the occasion."

In the end, one was chosen of which all approved. They arranged themselves, the men at the front and the women at the back. Caetano D'Costa, an elder in the congregation, making the sign of the cross, intoned at the top of his voice the first words of the Latin verse, *Deus ajutorum meum intende*, and the rest of them joined in, Ubald-Bab accompanying them on the fiddle. Outside, firecrackers exploded, announcing to the village that the *ladainha* had started, and as the *Kyrie eleison* began, latecomers hurried in.

When the first part of the ladainha was over, Ubald-Bab mopped his sweating face on the sleeve of his shirt. Others, too, complained of the heat and urged the fiddler to continue before they and the candles melted. He put the violin back to his shoulder and played some samples until the gathering chose the tune that they liked. Now the second part of the ladainha began and they sang *Salve Rainha* and *Mai de Deus*. To finish this part, Rosa requested them to sing a special hymn to the Holy Cross.

Now came the last phase of the ladainha. Caetano D'Costa knelt down and the rest of the congregation knelt with him. He led them through many repetitions of Our Fathers and Hail Marys for the departed souls of the Jaques' household. The congregation was relieved when it came to an end. It was, though, not quite finished, because Rosa requested Caetano D'Costa to say more prayers. He looked at her curiously, but did as he was asked. Then firecrackers were exploded again and the ladainha was over. Now the festivities began. The notables and others of the *chaddo* caste sat in the *sala*, the others on benches out in the balcony. *Maceira* was brought in fine glasses to the notables; for the rest, feni, the common man's drink, was served in goblets. The chaplain rose to his feet to raise the toast and all stood up with him, but the youngsters were still making too much noise for him to start.

"What kind of generation is this," Cursin complained. "You don't even know how to respect the chaplain!"

Cursin's reprimand at last brought silence and the chaplain began. He besought heavenly blessings on Rosa's son and pleaded with God to make him a good Catholic, though he was sure that he would be, if he followed his mother's example. When he'd finished his speech, the chaplain gulped his drink and a chorus of *vivas* rang through the room and the balcony. Many other toasts and many more *vivas* followed.

Then *soupa verde* was served, and after came *arroz refugado* with the topping of *sorpartel*. Mazancit beamed with joy when she heard the village notables praising her cooking. The guests ate and drank and talked. They talked about the infant Mario, the paddies and the unpredictable rage of the Goan monsoon.

"Don't worry," said Plough Francis loudly. "Didn't Ocobae's son unlock the doors of Heaven and bring rain on our parched earth? Do you think he'll allow the paddies to be flooded?"

The chaplain eyed him reproachfully.

"I want another drink," demanded Plough Francis, "I want to raise a toast to Ocobae and her son."

Cursin filled his goblet.

"Where is Ocobae?" demanded Plough Francis.

Rosa came from the kitchen and stood before him.

"Ocobae, your son is an angel," he said staggering on his feet, "You're the mother of an angel. He brought us rain and made our paddies green, he brought hope and joy into our hearts."

"Plough Francis is drunk," someone called out.

"I'm drunk because I'm happy," he said, gulping down the rest of his drink, "but mark my words!"

It was past midnight when the talk was exhausted. One by one the guests took leave. Out in the darkness frogs croaked, crickets chirped and fireflies flew like tiny lanterns in the night.

Inside, calm returned and Mazancit, Majakin, Concentin and other kitchen aides started their party. They ate and drank and talked about the success of the ladainha.

Rosa left them, feeling very tired, knowing that Modo-mai and others would finish off the things in the kitchen. Before going to bed, she gave Mario her breasts and then fell asleep by his side.

In the morning, Modo-mai Majakin awoke Rosa with some tea.
"Modo-mai..." said Rosa, "Oh, never mind... I'll be down in a
moment."

When she was dressed, Rosa opened her window and looked out.
It was drizzling. On the path to the paddies, she saw Plough Francis,
a pair of oxen, skeletal and obedient, trotting in front of him; on his
naked shoulder he was carrying a wooden plough. For a moment
Rosa stood in thought, faintly remembering the traces of a dream.
There was something about the scene that disturbed her.

CHAPTER VI

By mid-August the monsoon had abated and, on the day of the feast of Our Lady of Assumption, the chaplain led the faithful to the paddies, and a few sheaves were cut and blessed. This was the ceremony of thanksgiving.

This year there would be a bumper crop of rice; ponds and lakes were teeming with fish, the calm sea was already providing bountiful catches and the green earth was a grazing heaven to the cattle and pigs. Tar Menin and Hut João went about whistling and puffing on home-made cigars. In a few days, Tar Menin's buffalo-cow and Hut João's cow would be giving birth; and then, there would be plenty of milk in the village for those who could afford it. After the harvest, hens and ducks would be laying eggs and already vegetable gardens were yielding plenty; they knew that the fruits would be in abundance, too.

The ordinary folk of Cavelossim, though not the elite, put all this down to Mario. Whenever they passed Rosa's house, they called in to see him. Affection in their faces, they said, "Ocobae what would have happened to us if Mario-Bab hadn't come into this world?"

All this made Rosa feel as if Mario wasn't her son at all. Often, sitting on her balcony, giving Mario her breasts, tears streaming from her eyes, she would plead with the Holy Cross, "It's true that I begged you to give me a son. But please, I'm a woman, I'm a mother. Please don't take him away from me. Let him marry and beget children – lots of children. Please, please, don't take my son away from me. Don't make a saint out of him."

One afternoon Liban came and squatted by Rosa. Seeing her sadness, she asked, "Ocobae, why tears? Is something wrong with Mario-Bab?"

Rosa wiped her tears and said, "Oh, no! He's fine." Then to change the subject she asked Liban how the paddies were doing. "You weeded my fields very carefully this year and Hut João did a very good job of ploughing. God will reward you in Heaven."

"Ocobae, that's our duty," said Liban. "We are your mundcars and depend on you; if you are prosperous, there will be food in our bellies, if not, we'll starve."

"By the way," said Rosa, "will you call *mar*-Anton for me?"

"Of course."

"There are many baskets to mend and new mats to be made before the harvest. I hope she isn't too busy."

"Mar-Anton will make time for you, Ocobae. Don't worry about that."

Rosa knew that *mar*-Anton, an untouchable wouldn't let her down. Harvest time was the only occasion she could feel a little dignity when she was in demand to weave and mend the baskets and mats. But Rosa couldn't keep up her pretence of interest in the harvest for long, and Liban didn't miss her anxious glances at Mario.

"What's worrying you?" Liban asked. "Is it Mario-Bab?"

"No! No!"

"I'm looking forward to when Mario-Bab is bigger."

"Big?" screeched Rosa. "I want him always to be a child."

Liban smiled. "When he's a big boy, he can come and see the paddy being threshed. You'd like that wouldn't you, Mario-Bab?"

"Which child doesn't?" said Rosa.

This discussion ended abruptly when Liban cried, "Ocobae, I see a horse-carriage coming. Could it be Bab?"

"I don't think so," said Rosa.

But as the carriage came nearer, one of the village urchins who was climbing the carriage rails at the back, leapt off and came running to Rosa. "Ocobae, Bab has come all the way from Bombay to see Mario-Bab."

A smile bloomed on Rosa's face.

"Mario-Bab, your papa has come," said Liban. "Your papa must be dying to see you."

The carriage halted in front of the house and Liban ran onto the road to greet senhor Jaques.

"Bab! How are you, Bab?"

"I'm fine; and you, Liban?"

"Because you pray for me, Bab, I'm fine."

Maximiano Jaques paid the driver and climbed the stairs to the balcony. Liban, in the meantime, lifted the heavy trunks from the carriage and with the driver's help, carried them on her head into the house.

Rosa was standing with Mario in her arms, her heart fluttering as her husband approached. He looked at his son, the flesh of his flesh. He remembered how much he had longed to have his own child; now,

he was lucky enough to have a son. He had thanked the saintly souls
of his parents and those of his favourite saints for interceding on his
behalf. He held out his hands for his son and Rosa passed Mario to
him. Neither of them spoke, but tears rolled down their faces and
Liban wiped her eyes with the *palow* of her *capor*. Maximiano lifted
his son and looked at him. Which of them did he resemble? He hugged
him, the infant cheek pressing his. At that moment, the baby wet him.
"Look what he's done!" exclaimed Maximiano with a proud smile.

"That's a nice welcome your son gave you, Bab," joked Liban, as
she left to fetch another trunk and Maximiano went inside to change
his clothes.

The news of Maximiano's arrival soon spread in the village. Hut
João, Plough Francis, Mud Bosteão, Tar Menin, Oji-mai, Modo-mai
and many others came to congratulate him, and to all who came, he
offered feni, and those who were close to the family were given small
paper bundles containing tea and candy, brought from Bombay.

In the evening the village notables came to visit him. Sipping
maceira, senhor Tolentinho asked, "Tell us senhor Maximiano, what's
the news of Bombay?"

"The same."

"The same? Not any change after Gandhi's coming?" the chaplain asked, sipping maceira. "But things have changed for you. Tell
us, senhor Maximiano, have you thought what you want Mario to be?"

"No. Not yet."

"You must let Mario be a priest," the chaplain said.

"I don't have enough sons to give one to God."

"Offer to God the one you have. No son of Cavelossim has yet
become a priest," argued the chaplain. "If Mario becomes a priest,
he could elevate the chapel to a church."

"I can't do that with my only son!"

"Listen, senhor," said the chaplain, taking a sip of his drink, "if Mario
becomes a priest, your place and that of your wife is secured in Heaven.
What's the use of gaining the whole world and losing your soul?"

"Don't listen to him," butted in Tolentinho. "Becoming a priest
is out of the question. Who says that priests go to Heaven? We all
know about those who love their brothers' wives..."

The chaplain looked sour. What was senhor Tolentinho hinting at?

"Make a lawyer out of him," Tolentinho persuaded, "that's a
noble profession. If he became a lawyer, it would be a great honour
to Cavelossim."

"Why?" asked teacher Marcos.

"With legal knowledge Mario could fight to make Cavelossim a parish and elevate the chapel to the position of a church. That's why I want him to be a lawyer."

"No. Mario should never be a lawyer," argued the teacher. "Haven't we all seen the houses of lawyers? Their big mansions are almost in ruins and their homes are never blessed."

Maximiano, sipping his drink and smoking his pipe, was in deep thought.

"Lawyers are cheats," continued Marcos. "No good will ever come of making Mario a lawyer. When they die, the soil doesn't even eat them. You know why?" For a few moments the teacher kept quiet and then, declared, "Because they are corrupt. Isn't that so, senhor Tolentinho?"

Tolentinho looked uncomfortable and angry. All of them knew that one of his ancestors, a lawyer of sorts, had been a great cheat, acquiring lots of land by deceit. When his coffin was opened three years after his burial, the body was found to be unnaturally fresh, and though he was buried again, he never did rot. In the end, he was cremated, but even then his spirit wasn't released; it roamed in the village and made its home in a giant tamarind tree, frightening the people and possessing some. All this had convinced the lower castes that it was better to be poor, for in the end, they would inherit the Kingdom of God.

"If you don't want to make him a priest," said the chaplain returning to the conversation, "make him a teacher. It's a noble profession, too."

"You're all wrong," said Dr. Maurice. "What Cavelossim needs is a doctor. Who'll be there, when I am gone? Concentin? No. She doesn't know anything about medicine. Maximiano, listen to me. Let your son be a doctor. I'll pass on my medical secrets to him."

Maximiano began to yawn.

"You're tired," said Dr. Maurice, "and it's late. We better let you go to sleep."

"And you, Rosa," asked chaplain as he was leaving, "what do you want your son to be?"

"He'll be what God wants him to be," she said, bolting the door behind them.

CHAPTER VII

Cavelossim, in the district of Salcete, lay like a sleeping child in the embrace of the River Sal and the Arabian Sea. The River Sal came winding from a hill to Verna, passing through many villages. It had the appearance of a famished snake; reaching Cavelossim, it opened its mouth wide as if to devour the Arabian Sea, but instead it got swallowed up at Betul by the sea.

At low tide, at Cavelossim, the village women, mostly from the fisher caste, their *capods* hitched up above their knees, bent like flamingos, grazed the river bed for mussels; and then, baskets brimming, went from village to village, selling them. On the bank of the river, there are paddies, and beyond, coconut palms with other trees scattered among them. In the growing season, men and women were stooped amphibious creatures planting rice seedlings under the vigilant eye of a landlord or landlady standing among them with an open umbrella. In the coconut groves, the *kasti*-clad workers, sweat sparkling on their naked bodies, laboured with hoes under their landlord's scrutiny.

In those days, there was no fear of robbery, and no one bothered to bolt the doors and windows of their houses. God was the almighty feudal Lord who saw everything. In Goa, He was represented by the Portuguese Governor from Lisbon and the notables who ruled over the villages. Both were greatly feared. Goans lived in a paradise of peaceful subordination. In law, Cavelossim was neither a village nor a parish, but a *bairro*, annexed to the neighbouring village of Carmona. Though they had their chapel, they didn't have their own cemetery, because it wasn't a parish; and people from other villages with their own church and *communidade* would say, "Who are those people of Cavelossim? They're nothing but low-caste fisher-folk. Never let your daughter marry a Cavelossim boy. There are no families of good breeding there."

But Cavelossim had the makings of an independent village. It had a big enough population; it had *gaocares* from the chaddo caste; it had big landlords with *casa grandes* and it had wards of barbers, tailors, launderers and so on; but it had to function under the jurisdiction of Carmona parish and this was a humiliation.

Docile in many matters, village patriotism was the only political passion that aroused the people of Cavelossim. Such village politics weren't unwelcome to the colonial authorities. It kept the village intellectuals as big frogs in a little well.

Senhor Tolentinho Furtado was the leader of this movement, a staunch village patriot, a man who refused to stoop before any colonial official. Even his adversaries, the notables of Carmona, respected him for this. He was descended from a family with a history as ancient as that of the Portuguese Empire, an aristocrat whose ancestors had been amongst the first to embrace the Catholic faith. For this, they had been amply rewarded by the conquistadors with lands and prestige. Conscious of his place in the society, leadership was an instinct to senhor Tolentinho Furtado.

He lived in fading ancestral majesty in a huge mansion, the biggest house in the village. It had many big salons with layers of dust on their tiled floors and antique furniture. Portraits of Tolentinho's ancestors, with haughty expressions on their faces, hung on the walls. Dusty crystalline chandeliers dangled from the ceilings. The cupboards displayed the cracked but exquisite china from which his ancestors had eaten. In former days, Furtado's ancestors had given grand parties attended by colonial officials and even the Governor-General and the Bishop. In the yard at the back of the house a *machila*, relic of those days, rotted in the sun and rain. There were bedrooms with moth-eaten canopy beds where his ancestors had slept and made love. There were quarters for the servants, storerooms and granaries. It had a family chapel with a big altar on which stood a life-size Christ nailed to the cross. It was here that his ancestors had offered prayers for their good fortune.

Tolentinho was the only heir to the estate, which would have been ruined long ago had it not been for his widowed mother, who looked after the estate as an aristocrat should. When she had eventually died at ninety-five, Tolentinho's two sisters, who were *beatas*, had taken over its running. They had never married, villagers said, because their father wouldn't dower them with land. The estate, so far, had remained intact.

Tolentinho hadn't married either. Though his mother and sisters had pleaded with him to marry and beget an heir to the estate, he ignored their advice. The villagers, though, knew that he had fathered many illegitimate children with his mundcar women. Other aristocrats called him a liberal and predicted that his attitudes would bring his estate to ruin.

When evening fell, Tolentinho would stroll out from his mansion to join the other village notables. He was a tall hulk of a man with broad shoulders. As a notable, he wore white trousers and a white coat buttoned at the neck, leather *chinels* and a cap, which he doffed to the crosses he passed on the road. He swung a swagger cane to-and-fro as he walked. He was clean-shaven except for a wild untrimmed moustache, which enhanced his aristocratic hauteur.

On the main road, he would meet Dr. Maurice, teacher Marcos and other members of his clique, the less important tailing the acknowledged grandees as they strolled along discussing village politics. Their walk ended at the chapel's patio, where they continued their discussion until the bell rang for the angelus.

Tolentinho had penned many petitions to the colonial authorities requesting that Cavelossim become a separate village. Those who tailed the clique said he wrote Portuguese better than the Portuguese Governor himself, but neither the Governor's office nor the Bishop's had ever responded. He didn't know what else to do, or how he could stir up the villagers with a passion equal to his own. One day, he was in a state of such drunken despondency it brought tears to the eyes of Tar Menin, his mundcar. He had to do something to cheer his master up.

"Bab," said Tar Menin, humbly, "give me a sturdy buffalo bull."

Tolentinho looked at him blankly.

"If you give me a buffalo bull, Bab," he explained, "I'll train it into a fighter. Then it can challenge Baltazar-Bab's bull."

Baltazar Afonso was a notable of Carmona. Like many notables in those days, he had a passion for bull fights and was known all over Goa for his buffalo bull – a ponderous and ferocious beast which had never lost a battle. Baltazar had named it after his village.

Though Tolentinho had little hope that it would work, he felt he had nothing to lose and gave Tar Menin a sturdy young beast which he named Cavelossim. For a year, Tar Menin trained the bull in all the tactics of the fight.

"Bab," he told Tolentinho one day, "the Bull Cavelossim is ready."

The next day, Tolentinho issued a challenge to Baltazar. The latter readily agreed, having no doubt that his bull would win, and glad of another opportunity to humiliate the people of Cavelossim.

Soon Pedo, the village crier, went through Carmona beating a drum.

"Is someone dead?" villagers asked.

"No. Someone is going to die."

"Stop joking. Who's going to die?"

"Don't you know?" the crier said, "Baltazar-Bab's bull is going to slaughter Tolentinho-Bab's bull."

The villagers laughed and he told them when the combat would begin and where.

"You'd better ask the chaplain of Cavelossim to be there," one of the villagers said.

"Why's that?" the crier asked.

"To administer extreme unction, of course!"

The combat was held in Cavelossim, on a fallow field behind the chapel. People from Carmona, Cavelossim and neighbouring villages came pouring in. Spectators jostled for positions and youths climbed tall trees and coconut palms for a better view. As they waited, noisy arguments broke out as bets were made. Suddenly, there was silence as Tar Menin brought Bull Cavelossim into the field, and soon after, Terror Catean, Baltazar's manager, followed with Bull Carmona. The nooses from the bulls were taken out and they were worked up for the fight.

Bull Carmona stared arrogantly at Bull Cavelossim, scooping earth furiously with his hind legs; he was ready for the battle.

"Come on Carmona! Come on!" half the spectators shouted.

Urged on by this clamour, Bull Carmona was in a real rage. His neck muscles bulged. But Bull Cavelossim was calm, his eyes fixed on his opponent. Senhor Tolentinho watched anxiously. Was this a huge mistake? If Bull Carmona won, Baltazar would taunt him ever afterwards. If that happened, Tar Menin would certainly get a beating. He turned to see Baltazar close by him with a confident smile on his face.

At last, the battle began. Bull Carmona pawed up more earth and rushed head-on in attack. Bull Cavelossim shifted his position, throwing Bull Carmona off balance. At that moment, Bull Cavelossim got behind Bull Carmona and drove his horns deep into Carmona's rump. Carmona, his rump bleeding, was enraged, and he whirled about and thrust at Cavelossim with such force that he was sent backwards shaking his head. But he didn't give way. Bull matched bull and the earth tore under their hooves as they made several head-thrusts at each other. The spectators howled.

"Finish him off! Finish him off!" shouted Tolentinho and the villagers of Cavelossim.

Tar Menin's tricks hadn't gone to waste. Bull Cavelossim suddenly changed his position, and Bull Carmona, who had maintained his position for a long while, faltered and almost slumped to the ground. Incensed, Cavelossim rushed behind Carmona, stabbing him vigorously with his horns, tearing into the flesh, streams of blood gushing out. Carmona escaped the battlefield and ran through the paddies, Cavelossim in pursuit.

Tolentinho flung his cap into the air. He had never been so happy. Baltazar was crestfallen. What Tolentinho's years of petitioning couldn't accomplish, Tar Menin's strategy had achieved. He had so raised the pride of Cavelossim that there was now no way that they would remain subjected to Carmona. To get through to the common man, one must think like the common man – that's what Tolentinho learnt.

"Look at that chicken run!" shouted Tolentinho.

"But Bab," shouted his fellow villagers, "what can one expect from the people of Carmona? Don't worry, Bab, we will drive them away and make Cavelossim a parish. You can count on us."

Villagers talked about the fight for days. In Carmona they said that Tar Menin had administered something to their bull to weaken him. In Cavelossim, village patriotism, like a torch of palm leaves, burned in many hearts. Tolentinho knew that the fight to make Cavelossim a separate parish had begun.

CHAPTER VIII

The sleeping dragon had awakened. The villagers of Cavelossim wanted action but all senhor Tolentinho could come up with was a protest letter, written in Portuguese, arguing that Cavelossim should be a separate parish. This was circulated in both the villages and nailed on the portals of the Carmona Church. This, of course, irritated the notables of Carmona, though they couldn't help but appreciate the eloquent idioms that Tolentinho had used. Tar Menin, however, suspected that his landlord had written it less in hope of action than as a way of showing his ability in Portuguese and provoking a flush of anger on the faces of Carmona notables. If this was all it did, the awakened dragon would go into slumber, again. Something more drastic was called for.

Tar Menin didn't confide his plan to anyone, not even to senhor Tolentinho. He alone would execute it and he alone would take the responsibility. If caught, he wouldn't flinch, even when tortured. This way, he would be an inspiration to others.

He chose Saturday night to act. It was a starless night. As he passed Joseinho's taverna, he heard labourers talking over their drinks. He recognised some of the voices and hurried on. He met a few people on the way and with a disguised voice responded to their *bonnots*. At last he arrived at Carmona.

Baltazar Afonso's house was as big as Tolentinho's, though Tar Menin was sure his landlord's house was the biggest and his landlord the wisest. For him senhor Tolentinho was a king and he was his loyal and obedient subject. Tar Menin had formulated his own constitutional theory – if the king doesn't act in his own interests, his subjects must.

Baltazar's house stood alone, away from the main road. It was surrounded by giant coconut palms; at its back lay the River Sal.

He left the pathway as he was approaching Baltazar's house. He didn't want to leave his footprints, nor come across anyone who

might recognise him. Nearing the house, he hid behind a huge
mango tree. The lights in the house were still on. Goan notables
didn't go to bed early. Voices could be heard. The wall-clock struck
and he counted the strokes. Eleven.

"Damn it," he said, "it's still early."

After some time, Tar Menin heard the labourers leaving and then
Dona Matilda, Baltazar's widowed mother, shouting, "Baltazar, it's
time for rosary. Do you hear me?"

"Yes, Mama."

Though Baltazar was in his forties, married, with two grown up
sons and a daughter, he was still afraid of his mama.

The rosary started. Tar Menin heard Baltazar saying the decade
loudly and fervently. God must be deaf, he thought. Why did landlords
pray, he mused. They have everything. They must be praying to
cleanse their rotten souls. Do they ask God to give them power to
seduce the serf women and enjoy the pleasures of bed? Their souls
stink like their latrines.

But if Tar Menin didn't include senhor Tolentinho in these
complaints, he knew exactly what Baltazar was: a short, fat man, with
a flabby face, who often wore baggy suits like a clown in a circus;
a bully who would often burst into rage without any reason at the
sight of the common people; a miser who demanded gifts from the
serfs and made them work on his land without giving them a penny;
a man who lent money without a licence, at outrageous interest, and
grew fat on the pawned gold ornaments. Truly he was a pig, fattening
himself while the common man struggled to survive.

"Oh God, why are the wicked so powerful?" Tar Menin remembered his late mother. She had pawned her only pair of gold earrings
for a mere five rupees with Baltazar. She needed the money when Tar
Menin was taken to the doctor. "Mother, when I grow big," he'd said
as a boy, "I'll release your earrings." He remembered how his
mother had smiled. It still touched him and made him angry. He'd
saved every penny he could when he started working, and when he'd
collected enough, he'd gone to Baltazar and asked him to release the
earrings. "This isn't enough," Baltazar had told him. "This won't
even make the interest of so many years. Come with more."

The following year, when he had come with more money, Baltazar
had opened his ledger and had shown him that he still had more to
pay. He had come once more to Baltazar, and again, the earrings
weren't released. The money still wasn't enough. After his mother's

death, Tar Menin gave up on the earrings, but he silently cursed Baltazar and his offspring for generations to come. If God didn't want to teach Baltazar a lesson, he would.

But he could still hear Dona Matilda saying the decade in Portuguese. He wondered: Is it because the notables say their prayers in Portuguese that God makes them prosperous? Then, in the midst of the decade, Dona Matilda yelled, "Terezin! Terezin! Are you sleeping?"

Terezin was Dona Matilda's *posug*, adopted into the household as a child, and now their maid of all work.

"Go to the stable and check on Bull Carmona, and don't forget to close the portal when you come in," Dona Matilda growled.

From his hideout Tar Menin watched Terezin coming out with a flickering kerosene light, going into the stable and after a while returning to the house. A few steps away from the stable, stood a mountainous hayloft. Tar Menin hurried to it, and set a lit match to its bottom. The hay was dry and when he was certain that the fire had taken hold, he ran away as fast as he could.

Coming to the river, he plunged into it and swam to the other side, and from there, with the delight of a child, he watched the inferno. He was sure that he had done nothing wrong. If God was lazy or too busy, he had the right to dispense justice to a louse like senhor Baltazar. Apart from his personal motives, Tar Menin had political intentions. Now the notables of Carmona would definitely accuse the villagers of Cavelossim of this criminal act; and there would probably be retaliation from the villagers of Carmona. The colonial authorities would be forced to investigate the causes of these clashes and, eventually, Cavelossim would earn the status of a separate village.

It was around two in the morning when Tar Menin arrived home. Before going to lie down on his mat, he drank a pint of feni and sat wondering how senhor Baltazar would be taking the fire. He hadn't seen a notable faced with disaster. Had they feelings like the poor? Had the stable burnt too and roasted his cattle? If that happened, senhor Baltazar would be served right.

Tar Menin slept easily and when he woke up next morning at his usual early hour, the night was behind him. He made himself a mug of tea, sipped it calmly, then went to his stable to feed his buffaloes. There as usual, he met Lucian, collecting dung in a basket. She served the villagers by coating the earthen floors of their houses with cattle dung.

"Do you know, Menin," she said, "someone set fire to Baltazar-Bab's hayloft!"

"Who could do such a wicked thing?"

"I don't know."

"It's wicked! It's a crime! How can one see Baltazar-Bab's cattle starving? God will send a thunderbolt on such a person."

Lucian picked up her basket and went on her way. Tar Menin left for the Sunday mass, and on the way to the chapel, many told him about the fire. Though many condemned the act, he knew that they approved it in their hearts. The notables though, even those of Cavelossim, were united in their condemnation, and the chaplain threatened that if someone from Cavellosim was the culprit, God would starve them by a pestilence or a drought.

Baltazar, who suspected that senhor Tolentinho was behind it, inspected the whole place for footprints. Some fresh prints were discovered leading to the river, and Baltazar gave orders to cover them. Suspicion throbbed in his mind that Tolentinho's lackey, Tar Menin was the culprit. Though he fumed with rage, he didn't think it wise to lay his hands on Tar Menin, yet.

Baltazar, wanting convincing proof, held the rite of *supa-kator* in his prayer-room. His two trustworthy serfs, held a *sup* – a winnowing-pan woven out of bamboo threads – with a pair of scissors' blades hooked to it, pointing to the ground, supporting it on their fingers, through the scissors' loops.

Dona Matilda began the ritual by intoning Our Fathers and Hail Marys; in all, thirteen of them, to Saint Anthony. After this phase was over, Baltazar called out the names of suspects, one after the other. When Tar Menin's name was called out, the winnowing-pan rotated on the blades, as if it had its own will. Baltazar's eyes brightened. But he wanted to be absolutely sure about Tar Menin's crime.

On the table, facing the oratorio, he placed a black breviary, on the top of which, exactly on its middle, he placed a long iron key, its head pointing north. Once again, Dona Matilda said the same number of Our Fathers and Hail Marys to Saint Anthony, and the key on the breviary moved when Tar Menin's name was called. Now, he was sure who the culprit was and his hands itched to torture Tar Menin.

"Tar Menin has become too bold," he said to his mama. "Senhor Tolentinho is the cause. How can he take the common people in his confidence?"

When the news got to him that he had been found guilty at the Baltazar's house in the sessions of supa-kator and breviary, Tar Menin resisted the temptation to bolt away. He would bear all the tortures, he would never admit that he lit the fire.

The next evening, Cabo Noronha, the local police officer, came to arrest Tar Menin. He didn't put up any resistance nor show any surprise.

"Come here, *malandro*," Noronha shouted angrily at Tar Menin, slapping him, handcuffing him, and then marching him to the police station at Orlim. There, Cabo Noronha, getting drunk, interrogated Tar Menin. "You put the fire to the hayloft; didn't you?"

"No."

"Liar! *Filho da puta!*" Cabo Noronha lashed Tar Menin's naked back with his *cavalmarinha*.

Who are you calling a son of a whore? I'm not a mistiço, a half-caste mongrel like you, Cabo Noronha. Though he didn't express these thoughts, they passed through his mind, and Cabo Noronha, as if reading them, whipped Tar Menin until his arm ached and then had him thrown into a cell.

Next morning, Tar Menin was dragged to Baltazar's estate. Villagers and the notables from both villages were there.

"*Bom dia*, senhor Tolentinho!" senhor Baltazar called.

"*Muito bom dias!*" responded senhor Tolentinho.

The sight of Tar Menin, his hands cuffed at the back, looking defiant, but with tears in his eyes, tugged at Tolentinho's heart. His mundcars were like his children, and though he might shout at them and beat them sometimes, he wouldn't allow others to lay a finger on them. Tar Menin was a good mundcar. What proof was there against him? The footprints? They could be anybody's; yet it would be hard to prove Tar Menin's innocence.

"But Bab," said Tar Menin, "I didn't do it."

"I believe you; I'll do what I can," Tolentinho comforted him.

Tar Menin was dragged to the footprints and ordered to place his feet into them; when he did, they fitted.

"You, liar!" exploded Baltazar, slapping Tar Menin on the face. He didn't even wince. Baltazar raised his hand again.

"Lay off!" shouted senhor Tolentinho, lifting his cane. "Or I'll crack your skull, senhor Baltazar."

"What!" yelled senhor Baltazar, surprised. "Do you favour the criminal? Are you an accomplice too?"

"Shut up, Baltazar!" Tolentinho growled. "The footprints don't prove a thing." He looked at Baltazar's feet; they too might fit the prints; there could be many in the crowd with feet the same size. He asked Baltazar, "Would you be kind enough to put your feet in those footprints?"

"What a preposterous idea!" Baltazar snorted. "Whoever heard of anyone setting fire to his own hayloft? What do you take me for?"

"Will you please put your feet into those footprints?"

"No!"

"Why not? Are you afraid, senhor Baltazar?"

"Put your feet into those footprints," said Dona Matilda, who so far had kept quiet. "You've nothing to be afraid of, my son."

Taking his feet out of his sandals, he placed them in the footprints. They fitted.

"You are the one who set fire to the hayloft, senhor Baltazar," Tolentinho accused.

"You are crazy, senhor Tolentinho," shouted Dona Matilda. "I can vouch for my son's innocence."

"How can you prove that, Dona Matilda?"

"Because at that time he was in the family chapel."

"I believe you, Dona Matilda. And I also believe that Tar Menin didn't set the fire, either."

"Tar Menin did! Tar Menin did!" Baltazar screamed.

"Why do you say that?"

"Because we had the rite of supa-kator."

"That mumbo jumbo?" asked Tolentinho.

"The winnowing-pan rotated against the name of Tar Menin. Saint Anthony would never tell a lie."

"Indeed, he wouldn't, would he senhor Baltazar?"

"What are you getting at?"

"Let's have another supa-kator ritual before all these people, senhor Baltazar, and see how many gold ornaments you took away from them."

"*Merda!* Get out, senhor Tolentinho!"

"Why? Are you afraid, senhor Baltazar?"

"If Menin didn't do it, who did?" said Dona Matilda loudly, looking at the crowd. There were few who liked her son; looking at them, she knew that they wouldn't rule out her son doing it himself. "I think I know how it happened," she said at last.

Baltazar looked at his mama. What was she up to?

"How, Dona Matilda?" demanded Tolentinho.

She explained that she had sent Terezin, her *posug*, to the stable to check on Bull Carmona. Soon after she had come into the house, they heard people shouting, "Fire! Fire!" and then, Girgirem, their mundcar woman, had come running and furiously knocked on the door shouting, "Ocobae, your hayloft is on fire, come out!"

"What do you suggest? Terezin set the fire?" asked Tolentinho.

"No. Not deliberately."

"You mean, it's an accident?"

"Exactly."

"How?"

"She was carrying a kerosene lamp, you know? And you never know with such things; an ember from the wick might have been carried away by the wind, landing it in the hayloft. I'm convinced that Menin never set the fire. Baltazar, set Menin free."

Tar Menin felt genuine gratitude and thanked Dona Matilda as he took leave.

But that night, he got drunk at Joseinho's taverna, and afterwards the whole village heard him as he went up and down the village road shouting the most obscene words, cursing Baltazar.

CHAPTER IX

Though Tar Menin burned to let the villagers know who had lit the torch to this rebellion, he knew he could never reveal his act; nevertheless, he would keep a vigilant eye on the progress of the fight.

It was senhor Tolentinho who reaped the rewards of popularity for the way he had protected Tar Menin from Baltazar. Such adulation boosted his morale and he wrote more pamphlets accusing the notables of Carmona of pocketing the income of Comunidade and Fábrica, without any benefit to Cavelossim. "And we know," he wrote, "that the pockets of senhor Baltazar are always bulging with the loot..."

Baltazar boiled at this insolence. What right had Tolentinho to accuse him like that? How had Tolentinho's forefathers amassed their riches? And who was Tolentinho? – An idiot, masquerading as a man of the people. He had to be taught a lesson.

Not long after, Tolentinho was woken early in the morning by an urgent knocking on his door. It was Tol Santan, one of his serfs.

"Bab," he said in distress.

"What's the matter? What brings you here so early?"

With tears in his eyes, Tol Santan stammered, "Someone has cut down the young coconut palms."

"What! How many?"

"All of them! All of them! It's a pitiful sight, Bab!"

Senhor Tolentinho had been expecting retaliation from Baltazar; he was only surprised at its delay.

"He's digging his own grave," he exploded.

"Who Bab?"

"Who else? Baltazar!"

Tol Santan was stupefied. How could one stoop so low? Though the land might belong to the landlord, he had planted the coconut seedlings with his own hands; he had made barriers around them to protect them from stray cows and goats; his wife had watered them; he had looked after them tenderly, as if they were his own children. And when they were about to fruit, they were cut down! The slashing of the young coconut palms was like slitting the throats of innocent youngsters. The whole of Cavelossim was indignant. .

Cursin, a thin, short young man from Cavelossim, a jack-of-all-trades, whose work took him to many villages, had a small crowd around him. "I went to Carmona to do a paint job," he was telling them. "I heard Monkey José's wife cursing our Tolentinho-Baba."

"Who's Monkey José?" they asked.

"Baltazar-Baba's mundcar."

"Why was she cursing our Tolentinho-Bab?"

"Her husband is arrested. People saw him dragged like a pig to the police station. Even Baltazar-Bab is taken there."

"Hope they beat him up," said Tar Menin.

"They only beat people like us," said Cursin.

The fact was that senhor Tolentinho had filed a suit against Baltazar and Monkey José and some other serfs of Baltazar had been arrested as suspects, beaten up at the police station and then released. Now the fight had gone to the court; the people of Cavelossim thought that they had won the first round of the fight. But the Goan courts processed cases with as much urgency as a sleepy python digesting a goat.

As the years went by, more recriminations followed between the two villages. But Cavelossim still wasn't a separate parish. In other parts of the region, villages became embroiled in various forms of local strife. At Varcá, two villages, away from Carmona, the sudras demanded that they be included amongst the pallbearers when the miraculous Christ was taken out in procession. But the gaocares argued that it was their inalienable right and they wouldn't share it with the sudras. The sudras argued that all men were equal in the eyes of God and they too had a right. Bitter clashes broke out with neither side wanting reconciliation.

Though there was an increase of minor disorder in the villages, the Colonial Government wasn't greatly concerned. As long as Goans were divided from each other, they wouldn't see beyond their separate cages. But into this confusion came the voice of Menezes Bragança. He preached the common humanity of mankind and urged Goans to shed their prejudices and think for themselves. It was a voice in the wilderness. Only a few were open to his message and they were in no position to act. And so the Colonial Government and the landlords kept the Goan masses in Paradise where none did any thinking of their own.

BOOK II

CHAPTER X

Mario, like most village children, was often ill. His head wrapped in a white shawl, Rosa carried him on her hip or sometimes walked with him, holding his hand, to Dr. Maurice's dispensary.

"What's wrong with Mario-Bab?" anxious villagers would ask and Rosa would recite his medical history. Mario's face would sparkle with glee.

Of course, no one relied on Dr. Maurice alone. Rosa often consulted Oji-mai Concentin when Mario was ill. Her home-remedies were efficacious, but before prescribing them, she always insisted that the child's stomach should be cleansed. Her preferred purgative was an enema, and when Rosa administered one to Mario, he would bring the roof down. Afterwards, squatting to ease himself near the compound wall, he would scream even louder.

"What is it, Mario?" Rosa would ask. "Is the pig troubling you?"

"No, Mama."

Rosa knew. It was worms.

"That's good. They are coming out," she would comfort him. "Now you'll feel fine."

When Mario had finished purging, Rosa would clean him, bring him in and give him a bath; after that she would give him a tot of feni seasoned with bitters. Mario would make a face.

"That's for the worms," Rosa would say. "Drink it; otherwise they'll trouble you."

On Oji-mai Concentin's advice, Mario wore a collar with beaten garlic, knotted to a piece of cloth. He hated its smell, but Oji-mai said, "That smell will keep the worms from breeding in your stomach and you'll see how healthy you are!"

After sunset, Rosa would sit in her doorway with Mario in her lap, teaching him his catechism. That over, Mario would say his prayers very loudly:

God make the coconut palms fruitful
Bless the paddies with good harvest
Make the sea bountiful with fish
Above all, bless us all with good health,
And God, bring peace to our village.

One day Mario got ill, very ill. He had a high fever and convulsions. Froth came from his mouth and sometimes he vomited. When he rolled his eyeballs upwards, Rosa brought the whole village running with her desperate cries for help. Dr. Maurice tried all that he knew but his efforts were of no avail. He sent for Dr. Antonio Colaço, an expert, who examined Mario and prescribed medicines, but nothing helped. Mario hovered between life and death. Oji-mai Concentin put water compresses on his head to bring the fever down, applied rice poultices, drenched his head with onion juice and did all that she knew; and yet Mario wasn't getting any better.

The villagers prayed for him and made vows to their saints. Modomai vowed that if Mario recovered, she would take him on foot to Varcá to visit the miraculous Christ, light candles to Him and give Mario *lavatorio* to drink. Yet Mario wasn't getting any better. He lay listless, his mind wandering, and sometimes tears trickled down his cheeks.

"You aren't going to die," said Oji-mai firmly. She hadn't forgotten the day she had yanked him from Rosa's womb.

Oji-mai's forehead was deeply furrowed. "Could it be?" she wondered aloud.

"Could it be what?" Modo-mai Majakin asked.

"Dist?"

"But whose evil-eye?"

"That we have to find out."

Mario had always worn a trinket on his gold chain, a present from his godmother, to protect him from evil-eye. But even so, one could never tell. Modo-mai went about the village enquiring, and villagers remembered a beggar-woman going from house to house receiving fistfuls of rice. The unusual thing about her was that she was dressed in *vistido*, indicating that she came from a high caste family; she was neither a beggar nor poor. Others confirmed that she was from Benaulim and that she came from a brahmin caste. They remembered the sad story she had told. She was childless, though she had been married for ten years. She knew why. Her husband's inheritance was ill-gotten; they were cursed by those who had been wronged. She had offered masses to the departed souls of her husband's ancestors, yet she wasn't pregnant. To touch the divine heart, she had become a beggar; with a coconut shell for a begging bowl, she had gone from house to house.

"Do you remember a beggar-woman coming to your door?" Ojimai Concentin asked Rosa.

"There are so many who come."

"I mean, an unusual one, in a frock."

"Yes."

Rosa remembered her, and also her story – almost like hers. It had brought tears to her eyes. As Rosa was consoling her by telling her own story, Mario had happened to come out of the house. "That must be your child. What a beautiful child you have!" the beggar-woman had said.

"God will give you one too."

"A boy?" the woman had asked, with a devouring look at Mario. "Yes."

"You're lucky."

In the meantime Mario had gone to the pantry and scooped out a handful of rice from the container. Coming to the beggar-woman, he put it into her bowl.

"Join your hands, my little one, let me bless you," she said.

When Mario had joined his hands, she blessed him and said, "May you grow into a big boy."

She asked him to come closer and when he did, she ruffled his hair. "How I wish I had a son like you!"

It all came back to Rosa now. On the very night the beggar-woman had left, Mario had burnt with fever.

"But why my son?" Rosa lamented.

"Now we know that it's dist," Concentin said, "we can get rid of it."

Neuinta, Mario's godmother, was sent to Benaulim to seek out the beggar-woman. She discovered that she had a weakness for drink, befriended her, got her drunk and, without any difficulty, cut a piece from her dress – a vital ingredient to remove the dist.

Hut João, was despatched to Bardez to fetch Nelson D'Souza. It was said that one of his ancestors had been bestowed the gift of removing evil-eye by St. Thomas. When they returned, a tray with red chillies, salt and a chunk of alum was put before him.

"But where's the piece of cloth from the suspect's vestment?" D'Souza asked.

Rosa gave it to him and he held it in his hand, examining it very carefully. After that, taking each ingredient in turn, he traced the sign of the cross on Mario's forehead and then, all over his body. Reciting the Credo, he circled each ingredient above Mario's head, and then put them into a hollow tile containing glowing charcoal stones. The salt exploded and the room smelt of burning chillies and cloth.

"Come and look," Nelson called Oji-mai Concentin, as he removed the melted alum from the hollow tile.

The furrows on the forehead of Oji-mai Concentin deepened, and Rosa, taking the alum in her hands, declared, "It's the face of that beggar-woman, no doubt about it!"

Disticar Nelson ordered Mario to spit on it three times, and when he had done so, asked him to crush it under his left foot, until it turned into powder. The next day, Mario's fever had gone.

CHAPTER XI

By the time Mario was eight, he was healthy and robust, but Rosa didn't stop worrying about him. It was time for him to begin primary school. Maximiano Jaques wanted his son to achieve the high status that he had failed to gain. Having a son who was something would elevate his prestige, too. But at the Portuguese Primary School in Carmona, Mario was a big disappointment.

Teacher Marcos said he had never come across such a dullard. Even the sons of the lower castes, he said, had more brains than Mario. Marcos had a very high reputation as a teacher; he had polished the intellects of many of the village notables in their childhoods with his cane, and many of them, particularly those now in high government posts, were forever grateful for him. His candidates for *Primeiro Grau* and *Segundo Grau* examinations had never failed. But what could he do with such a blockhead?

Marcos couldn't neglect Mario as he did the children of lower castes. For them education wasn't that important; none of them would be given Government jobs; but Mario was a notable's son so it was his duty to do his best. With a long whip in his hand, like a lion tamer, Marcos drilled lessons into Mario but nothing went in. He whipped the boy mercilessly and made him kneel on sharp stones. Mario took all these punishments without shedding a tear, and with a faint smile on his face, as if he were untouched by the pain. This further enraged Marcos and he would shout at him in Portuguese, "You're nothing but a donkey!"

Maximiano Jaques was upset to learn from Marcos that Mario was a dunce. He had taken early retirement from his post so that he could guide his son in his studies, cultivate those with influence and, if necessary, bribe the examiners. He knew how the system worked. With the proper connections and the right bribes, even an idiot came out bright from these examinations. But deep down, Maximiano had a hunch that Mario wasn't a dullard. He was just a spoilt brat, spoiled by his mother with too much love. He instructed Rosa to be strict with Mario and he himself became more severe. He set out rules for Mario: the time to be at home, the time to be with his books, and the most important rule of all, that Mario should talk only Portuguese with his parents and other notables. His mother tongue, Konkani, he could use only when talking to the uneducated villagers.

Mario resented this regimentation, but he didn't rebel. In the early morning, sitting in the balcony, he could be heard conjugating Portuguese verbs: *"Eu amo, tu amas, ele ama..."*

But there was too much distraction at that hour. On the red dirt road that passed by his house, he saw bullock-carts loaded with building stones and heard their drivers singing and the bells on the oxen's neck jingling. Poetry filled his heart and he felt sorry for himself. He would see the village girls coming from the vegetable gardens, their wet dresses clinging to their skins. "What are you looking at?" they would tease. "Do your lessons." He would return to Portuguese verbs, but his mind was not there.

As the sun became brighter, he would hear his father calling him, "Mario! Bring your lessons." His heart would go tom-tom and his legs shake. His father, sitting in his armchair with a harsh look on his face and a cane in his hand would order, "Conjugate the present future of *partir*."

Stammering, Mario would conjugate, *"Eu partirei, tu partiràs..."*

"You don't stammer when you ask for food from your mama, do you?"

Mario would shake even more.

"Say it again, without stammering, you fool."

Mario would make mistakes, and more mistakes. His father's cane would come down on him without mercy. Though he shook all over, he never cried, but often lost control of his bladder. If Cursin was under the mango tree giving haircuts, he would plead with Maximiano not to cane Mario like that. And Neunita, Mario's godmother, if she was collecting pig droppings near Rosa's house, hearing Maximiano's outburst, would come running entreating Maximiano not to beat her godson.

"You've no right to interfere in my affairs. Get out!" Maximiano would bawl at them. But when his anger had subsided, he would say, "What am I supposed to do if he doesn't study?" And he would order Mario to begin all over again. But Mario would never get his verbs right; and Maximiano would beat him pitilessly.

"Stop that! Don't kill my son!" Rosa took the cane away from her husband. "I carried him for nine months; you didn't. He was given to us by the Holy Cross. Let him remain ignorant, if that's God's will."

When Mario wasn't selected for the *Primeiro Grau*, Maximiano felt humiliated. He begged Marcos but he argued that Mario was still young, that he might do better next year. That day, blind with humiliation and rage, Maximiano made good use of his cane. "I don't want an idiot son like you! Get out!" he snarled.

Mario, pants wet with urine, skin red with cane marks, but with no tears in his eyes, looked at his father.

"Get out! Get out!" Maximiano shouted again.

Rosa screamed, "He's my son! He's my son! He isn't going anywhere."

"You've spoiled him! You've tied him to your apron strings!"

Rosa knew her son's destiny; her husband did not. Putting her arms around Mario, she silently prayed to the Holy Cross and asked Him not to make her son a saint. She took him to his bed and undressed him. What a brute her husband was! The welts on Mario's skin had swollen and in some places the skin had torn and bled. She gently rubbed oil into his body.

That night Mario slept a deep, exhausted sleep. Rosa didn't call him for rosary nor for supper; she didn't want to disturb him, but she went now and then to his room to see if he was asleep. When, finally, she lay down by her husband, familiar thoughts came to plague her mind.

"No! No!" she cried out in her sleep.

"What is it Rosa?" Maximiano, awakened, asked.

"I saw a huge cross."

"A cross?" he yawned. "It's just a dream, Rosa; go to sleep."

Not being able to sleep, she went to Mario's room. His bed was empty. He must have gone to the toilet, she thought, and called out for him. But there was no response. She ran to the toilet and opened its door. He wasn't there. "Mario! Mario!" she shouted.

"What's the matter?" asked Maximiano.

"I think ..." Rosa couldn't even say it.

"Ran away? At this hour?" said Maximiano.

He was sure a boy as young as Mario would be afraid to go out in the dark and that he must be hiding somewhere in the house. They looked in every nook and corner, but couldn't find him. Rosa was shouting so loudly the whole village awoke and came running. Without wasting any time, Tar Menin, with a palm-leaf torch in his hand, went by the riverside with Cursin. Plough Francis and Hut João took the seaside direction. Ubald-Bab and some others went by the paddies.

The sun appeared on the horizon. Mario still hadn't been found. Though no one pointed fingers at Maximiano, tears were in his eyes, and he promised himself that he wouldn't lay a finger on Mario again. He pleaded, "God, bring back my son, bring him home, safe."

"Bab," Modo-mai Majakin called.

"Is Mario found?"

"Look on the door; there's something written."

They saw the words chalked: *PAPA, EU SOU MORTO ... Papa I'm dead.*

"Oh my God, what have I done?" cried Maximiano.

Modo-mai and Oji-mai Concentin, always calm in any tragedy, tried to console him. Oji-mai said, "Mario-Bab would never do such a thing. He's somewhere safe and sound. He'll be found."

At that moment, Cursin and Tar Menin appeared leading Mario by the hand. Rosa ran like a hare and wrapped him in her embrace and Maximiano heaved a sigh of relief. He said nothing to Mario, but neither did he embrace him.

"Actually, we didn't find him," Cursin explained. "It was Sirpad, the son of goldsmith Pondory – he'd gone to ease himself on the bank of the river – he saw Mario hiding in the bushes."

"You better give Mario some holy water to drink," Oji-mai advised, "you never know, a bad spirit might have come on him."

The chaplain came in his vestments and read from his fat breviary, sprinkling holy water on Mario.

"You know, Rosa," said the chaplain after the ceremony, "why don't I train Mario to be an altar boy?"

"Yes, Mama, I want to be an altar boy."

It was decided that Mario should be an altar boy; at least that would keep him away from trouble.

But Maximiano was still unhappy. He wasn't sure if Mario would be selected to answer the examination even the next year. Teacher Marcos still hadn't given any good reports. In despair, he turned to Cavelossim's other teacher, Apolinario Da Costa.

Apolinario wasn't as highly educated as Marcos, and besides, he didn't have a teaching licence. He taught the children of the lower castes, the rejects of the Primary School of Carmona. He agreed to tutor Mario, though Maximiano had grave doubts. How could someone who never used the cane get good results? But Apolinario taught with patience and love, and Mario began to improve under his tutorship, so much so that the next year he passed his *Primeiro Grau* examination in *optimamente habiltado*. Maximiano was jubilant and his grandiose aspirations for his son returned.

CHAPTER XII

But at Apolinario's school, Mario, gradually unfolding like a flower bud, was developing in a different way. The more he came to know the hardships of the poor and the families of the lower-caste children who attended Apolinario's school, the more he reflected. The chaplain and his godmother Neunita had taught him that God created man in His image. How could the lives of the rich and the poor be so different?

"Mother," he asked Rosa one day.

"What is it, my son?"

"Are we all children of Our Father?"

"Of course."

"Are we all equal in the eyes of God?"

"Indeed, we are."

"Then, mother, why are Oji-mai, Modo-mai and others like them and outcastes like Mar Anton treated as good-for-nothings? We don't treat them as equal to us, do we, mother?"

Rosa looked at her son. What sort of questions were these! For a moment he seemed to have left his childhood behind, though he was only twelve.

"God's ways are strange," she explained. "Even in Heaven there are superiors and inferiors, angels and archangels."

But Mario wasn't satisfied with his mother's answers. He went to the chaplain, thinking that he would be better informed. "God made the rich and the poor," explained the chaplain. "That's the way He made it. We have no right to question Him."

"Aren't we all children of Our Father?"

"We are," said the chaplain. "What's bothering you, Mario?"

"Nothing."

In the dead of night, alone in his bed, he would hear the sea breathing. He would lie there, disturbed by a flood of thoughts, trying to hear God's message. What does Our Lord's prayer really mean? What kind of will is carried out in the Kingdom?

The sea roared and the wind moaned through the trees and sometimes, he heard Ubald-Bab disturbing the silence of the night or Petu-Bab, the village drunk, shouting obscenities and cursing the village notables. But he would return to his thoughts and ponder,

"Give Us This Day Our Daily Bread." Wasn't this a warning for mankind not to be greedy?

By now Ermelin's rooster was crowing. Mario was awake again after a few hours of fitful sleep. Different thoughts came to his mind now. Why should he learn Portuguese? The more he thought, the more clear it became to him. Education made people pompous, made them look down on the poor. If they became officers in the Colonial Government, what did they do? Steal. Why should he become a thief?

He put his doubts to Apolinario. "Why should I become a thief?"

"You don't have to."

"But I'll become one."

"No, you won't, because you're different. Your mind won't be subordinated, not even by Colonial education. You'll always arrive at the real truth. Colonial education will just be a stepping stone, will open your eyes wider, and then your mind will blaze with visions and dreams."

Mario always had visions and dreams. He dreamt of a kingdom without a King and in that kingdom there were people very much like those on earth: people with different colours, shapes and sizes, the only difference being that there were no kings, nations or religions dividing them into bigoted groups, setting one against the other. Whatever they did, they did for the common good and the good of the planet. They had no thought to lay an axe on the root that sustained them. Why couldn't people on earth be like that?

While other boys of his age ventured out into the world, he withdrew like a tortoise into its shell. He was troubled by his thoughts and sometimes he brought strange questions to the chaplain, but the chaplain just laughed them off. He would fall on his knees before the saints in the chapel, seeking answers from them, but they never moved their lips; they stood there like dummies. He became despondent and, in despair one day, stole mass-wine from the sanctuary and got drunk on it and ate all the consecrated wafers from the chalice. As he staggered home, he shouted, "There is no God! There is no God!"

The whole village heard him. They were mortified.

"He's possessed!" the chaplain howled when Mario was brought to him the next morning. "There are demons in him!" The chaplain read from his black breviary. He dipped the sprinkler into the stoup and sprinkled holy water on Mario. But Mario just stared at him. The chaplain trembled, his voice swollen in anger.

"Get out, you demon get out!" he bellowed, lashing Mario with his sacred cord. "In the name of God, be gone!"

The whole village, who had come to see the exorcism, watched with intense curiosity. Only when the chaplain brought his crucifix closer to Mario's face did he respond.

"You're a hypocrite!"

"You call me hypocrite?" shouted the chaplain, the crucifix shaking in his hand. "You son of Lucifer!"

"What should I call you?"

"Reverend."

"Why?"

"Because I'm a man of God."

"Aren't we all?"

The chaplain was getting uncomfortable with Mario's eyes boring into him, as if undressing his soul. The priest was no longer sure if Mario was possessed by the Devil or God.

"You're nothing but a hypocrite!" announced Mario again.

The chaplain lashed him, but Mario didn't cringe, and looking deep into chaplain's eyes, he asked, "Don't your words say one thing and your actions another?"

The chaplain was stunned.

"Tell me Reverend," said Mario, "don't you preach every Sunday that there is no greater sin than the sins of the flesh? Don't you chastise the women in your sermons if they expose a bit of their flesh? Don't you condemn them to the depths of Hell?"

Senhor Tolentinho, who was in the crowd, knew what Mario was getting at. There was a rumour, spread by Pedo Betal, that Antoneta, a devout spinster, was seen in the chaplain's room now and then. Tolentinho sensed that Mario was going to expose the chaplain and, gentleman that he was, he wanted to save the chaplain from the shame.

"Enough of your interrogation," he said. "Go to your chapel."

In a daze, the chaplain collected his tools, conscious that the eyes of the crowd were on him.

The crowd dispersed and Rosa took her son home. Silently she prayed to the Holy Cross to guide their son to walk the traditional path as their forefathers had done.

In the morning, when Mario got up, he was silent and didn't touch his breakfast. Rosa was afraid that the demon hadn't left him. Many in the village had been possessed, though in most cases the evil spirits had been driven away. But a few had been unlucky. The evil spirits had killed them and possessed their souls. Rosa didn't want such a fate for her son. Rosa asked the chaplain to exorcise Mario again but he declined.

Rosa approached Tar Menin. He had driven away evil spirits from many; only a week ago he had driven one away from twenty year old Gloria. He was always ready to show his prowess and agreed to confront Mario's demon the next Sunday.

Sunday came and the people returned after mass to watch the spectacle. Tar Menin, with a big whip in his hand, demanded of Mario, "Tell me your name! Tell me your name!"

But Mario looked at him calmly.

"Don't get me mad!" shouted Tar Menin. "Don't make me use the whip! Tell me your name!"

The evil spirit in Mario stubbornly refused to say anything. Tar Menin's eyes bulged with rage and he whipped the spirit savagely. "This must be a stubborn one," he said, his voice hoarse, his hands aching.

"This must be José De Campos," said an onlooker. "Didn't we see how he defied our chaplain? Only José De Campos had spunk like that."

The spirit of José De Campos was said to be very malignant. He came from Varcá, two villages away from Cavelossim and as a youth he had been involved in an argument over who should be a pallbearer of the miraculous Christ in procession. He had insulted the vicar of the church and, a few days later, his mutilated body had been found in the church compound. Nobody knew who did it. Now his ghost lived up in a giant tamarind tree at the back of the cemetery of Varcá. But how could Mario be possessed by the spirit of José De Campos?

"Ocobae," asked Tar Menin, "did you take Mario-Bab to Varcá any time?"

"I did," said Modo-mai. "You remember? I made a vow to take Mario for the kiss of the miraculous Christ if he got well from his last sickness. I took him last Good Friday."

"How did you go?" Tar Menin asked.

"On foot."

"At what time of the day?"

"In the morning."

Modo-mai Majakin remembered. It was very hot and the road was burning like a furnace; all walked barefoot because it was Lent. Mario had complained that his feet were sore, but Modo-mai had turned a deaf ear, thinking that a little penance would be good for him. But afterwards, she had taken pity and given him his sandals to wear.

Approaching the church of Varcá, Modo-mai took Mario to a stall under the shade of a huge tamarind tree, at the back of the cemetery, where pilgrims were given free food and drink. After having rice-soup there, they went to the church, and were lucky to find a place inside. There they witnessed the re-enactment of Christ's Passion. Mario had been touched by the spectacle. It was a long day and the sun had gone down when they left to go home. On the way, Mario stumbled on a stone under the same tamarind tree and the lavatorio bottle that he had been given to carry home dropped from his hand and smashed into small pieces. Modo-mai had thought nothing about it until now.

"It's the same tamarind tree, the abode of José De Campos," said Tar Menin. "It's him; I'm sure."

Tar Menin did all he knew to expel José De Campos' spirit. He asked him: "Why have you come on Mario? Do you have a message to give to someone? Do you want your favourite food? Or do you want masses for your soul? What do you want?" José De Campos took all the flogging from Tar Menin but obstinately refused to answer his questions.

In the end, Mario was dragged to the tamarind tree at Varcá. Forcing him to the ground, Tar Menin pressed his foot on his neck, making him bite at the base of the tree. Then a gun was fired into the air and water was poured on him. Afterwards, Mario was stripped of his wet clothes and dressed in new ones. But he wasn't unconscious as he was supposed to be. Tar Menin couldn't be sure if José De Campos had left Mario.

CHAPTER XIII

A year went by.

Though the chaplain had dismissed Mario as an altar boy, he often saw him praying in the chapel when it was empty, his eyes fixed on the lit tapers. He didn't dare approach him for he was still not sure whether Mario was possessed by the spirit of God or the Devil.

Mario did very well in the *Segundo Grau* examination and passed easily without his father having to bribe the examiners. Maximiano was proud of his son. Mario's success also brought much prestige to Apolinario. In the eyes of the lower-castes, Apolinario was their *mestri*, a revered teacher. Marcos seethed with anger. It was to him that the villagers' respect should belong and not to that charlatan.

"He is *endo*, an illiterate," said Marcos when one of the notables had praised Apolinario during their evening stroll.

"But he worked miracles with Maximiano's son, whereas you couldn't do a thing with him," said senhor Tolentinho.

"One Mario doesn't prove that Apolinario is a better teacher, senhor Furtado. He is fit only to teach the children of fisher-folk and people like that. My record speaks for itself. I've polished so many stones into diamonds. Many of my students are *empregados*. Some went to Portuguese Africa, others have became doctors and lawyers. His students have become toilet cleaners on board the ships!"

"What Apolinario is doing is wrong," said senhor Flemingo Fonseca, a notable from Carmona. Fonseca spoke Portuguese in a mixed-up fashion, full of Konkani words and his intonation most un-Portuguese. Tolentinho often ridiculed him, but he was a practical man, adept in the art of patronage. Recently, the Colonial Authority had appointed him as Regedor. The appointment had gone to his head and he had turned into a real despot.

"What's wrong about it?" asked senhor Furtado.

"He has no right to open the eyes of the lower-castes."

"Are you afraid they'll talk better Portuguese than you?"

"You don't understand," said Fonseca, ignoring the remark, "if barbers' children and launderers' children learn to read and write, that's the way of God. They are born to serve us."

"Who says so?"

"That's the way it has always been and that's the way it always should be. You are a bachelor, senhor Furtado and you have no heir to your estate. You'll die and go. What do you care? But we have children, we have our sons and they have to carry our way to posterity. Apolinario must be stopped, and I'll see that he is."

Teacher Marcos sent school inspectors to harass Apolinario and he was taken to the police station and reprimanded. But Apolinario didn't care, he continued to teach the children of the poor under the shade of the trees, and Mario, to the indignation of the village notables, joined his tutor.

Marcos and Regedor Fonseca approached the chaplain and asked him to warn the congregation about Apolinario and Mario.

Next Sunday, in his homily the chaplain preached: "No children of yours should go to be instructed by Apolinario. Why do your children need reading and writing? Do you think that's going to take you and your children to Heaven? No. What your children need is to learn to earn their bread by the sweat of their brows. Reading and writing will not fill their bellies. Apolinario is insane, he isn't a teacher. How can you ever trust your children to him? Now I hear that Mario has joined Apolinario to teach your children. Only last year, Mario got drunk on mass wine and filled his stomach with consecrated wafers and went out shouting, 'There is no God!' How on earth can you trust your children to these two characters? How?"

Rosa, who was in the congregation, felt humiliated. Why was God doing this to her? Hadn't God shown that He was pleased at the arrival of her son? "God save my son, Holy Cross save my son," she pleaded.

The chaplain ended his homily, "If any one is seen associating with the devil-possessed Mario and that insane Apolinario, I'll deny them the last Sacrament; I'll not hear their confessions nor let them take Holy Communion."

"God save my son! Holy Cross save my son!" Rosa sobbed.

"What parents go through for the sake of their children!" whispered Dona Pelagia. "Pray to Our Lady, pray to the Holy Cross, and God will deliver your son from the devil. I'll pray too."

What could Rosa do? Simple woman that she was, devout woman that she was, she could take comfort only in prayers and without that consolation she would have gone insane. What hurt her most was her husband's affliction. He, once boisterous, had become painfully silent and withdrawn.

"It was more blessed to be without a son," he whispered on their conjugal bed.

Rosa took her husband to her bosom and, caressing him fondly, said, "Mario is our only son. We may not be able to impose our dreams on him. Our dreams may be stale. His dreams may be like new buds waiting to bloom."

"What are you talking about, Rosa?" he asked. "There are no new dreams. Man's dreams come only from one source, from our old expectations and traditions."

Rosa sighed. Mario was a thorn in her flesh, yet he was her son; and thinking of Mario, she caressed her husband, who gradually slept in her embrace like a baby.

The villagers took the chaplain's warning seriously; theirs was the way of obedience, even though it troubled them not to keep up their communication with Apolinario.

Apolinario's role as mestri was finished; to earn his living, he left by train one morning for Bombay. Among the many he had taught, only Mario came to the railway station. As he watched his mestri board the train, Mario felt very lonely.

In time, Mario grew at ease with his own company, quite unconcerned that the village had boycotted him. But his visions of Paradise came haunting him, and the more he pondered them, the more convinced he was that the notables blocked the way to Paradise. A path had to be created. But how?

One day, Mario received a letter from his mestri; he read it avidly. His tutor advised that he shouldn't slacken in his studies, and Mario was glad that he hadn't let Apolonario down. Despite all the setbacks, Mario was doing well in his studies at the Institute of Abade Faria. His mestri had become a *tarvoti*; he would write him from every port in which he docked.

That night, thinking about his teacher and his journeyings, Mario felt the urge to get out of the house. He opened the window and slipped out. As he walked, he looked at the moon, round, bright yellow, and at the countless stars.

He walked until he came to the *Casa de Comunidades* at Carmona. There he heard a commotion. His feelings of being at one with the cosmos vanished. Who could be making such disturbance at this hour? Suspecting thieves, he hid behind a huge mango tree and watched. Soon he heard whispers. One voice was familiar. It was Baltazar's, the President of the *Casa de Comunidades*. What was he doing there? Then another person came into view in the moonlight; it was Flemingo Fonseca. They were up to no good. Soon he saw two of Fonseca's mundcars carrying away baskets of paddy on their heads.

This was the paddy that had been collected as taxes, one sixth of the produce, and stored in the *Casa*. Often Mario's mother hid part of the paddy. Mario remembered that he had accused her of cheating.

"Don't worry, they are bigger cheats," his mama had said.

"When the big people are cheats and thieves," Mud Bosteão had agreed, "what can you expect from the rest of us? We have to survive, you know?"

The next Sunday in the church and in the chapel, both the priests condemned the stealing of the paddy and pronounced that the thieves would be cast to the bottom of Hell, where they would burn and burn forever and ever.

"Whoever has stolen this paddy," said one *gaocar*, "I curse him forever; he has drunk our sweat and blood."

"But, I tell you, Bab," said Tar Menin, "this is an inside job."

The news of the theft soon spread in both villages. People were curious to find out how the paddy had been stolen this time.

"They came through the roof this time," said Baltazar.

"See the roof," said Regedor Flemingo, "a few tiles are missing. Through them they stole the paddy."

"Very clever thieves!" remarked the chaplain. "Hope we catch them this time."

"We will," said senhor Baltazar, "Regedor Flemingo and I will do our best."

"I hope you have better success this time," said the vicar.

The previous year, Baltazar had claimed that he had overworked for the good of the village, and had forgotten, in his tiredness, to lock the main door of the *Casa*. How the thieves came to know about this negligence, nobody knew; but all the tax-collected paddy was gone, and he was in anguish.

"It's an inside job!" Tar Menin was shouting.

There were others who shared Tar Menin's suspicions but they weren't so vociferous, with the exception of Petu-Bab, the village drunk, who went tottering up the road at night, shouting, "Who other than the notables stole the paddy? They will drink your blood, as I drink feni."

Baltazar and Flemingo had to invent culprits, otherwise suspicions would stick to them. Baltazar had an old grudge to settle with

Tar Menin, and there were other notables who would be only too pleased to see his potentially rebellious spirit squashed. Petu-Bab also had to be brought to book. And why not Mar Vincente, who lived close to the *Casa*?

Regedor Flemingo headed the Inquiry. President Baltazar, the vicar, the chaplain and Paxião Rodrigues, a less important notable of Cavelossim joined him. Tolentinho Furtado wasn't included; he wasn't to be trusted. They sent out the summons for Tar-Menin, Petu-Baba and Mar Vicente.

For days the inquiry dragged on as people assembled outside the *Casa* listening to and commenting on the proceedings.

"Why don't they just condemn them and finish it off?"

"They're shrewd. They want to give the impression that they're investigating it thoroughly."

"Be careful, don't talk like that."

The evidence was inconclusive, though many villagers were called in to give testimony. By now, the feast of the Holy Cross was approaching and people's interest in the trial was beginning to wane. But then, one morning, posters appeared nailed to the portals of the chapel of Cavelossim and the church of Carmona. They were beautifully hand-drawn and all too recognisable as the faces of the village notables in all their big-bellied splendour.

"That's Flemingo-Bab, our Regedor, isn't it?"

"That's Baltazar-Bab for sure."

"There's Paxião-Bab Rodrigues, too."

"And that's the vicar; and that one? The chaplain!"

"And what's that hanging from their necks?"

"That's their badge of honour."

"What does it say?"

"*Ladrão*. Thief."

The same kind of posters were pasted up at the market places of Carmona and Cavelossim, and before they were ripped down, most of the villagers had seen them and enjoyed them.

The members of the Committee of Inquiry were enraged. They loosed their anger on Tar Menin, Petu-Bab and Mar Vincente, but they knew it wasn't the work of those idiots. For the time being the inquiry was suspended and they devoted all their energies to finding out the author of the posters.

It was the time of Vespers of the Holy Cross, and this year the feast was being sponsored by Aquino Martins and his brothers. Aquino had gone to British East Africa, had made a fortune in diamonds and now he and his brothers were celebrating the feast with a splendour never before seen in the village. The villagers, indeed, were calling this the Feast of the Four Brothers. The main attraction was to be a spectacular display of fireworks. Word had spread and relatives of the villagers were pouring in. A band was already playing and at the *feira* the smell of roasting *gram* was in the air, as the youngsters moved from stall to stall choosing the presents they would ask their relatives to buy for them. Pigs squealed as they were carried on the bamboo poles to the slaughter. In the kitchens, women were busy at their grinding stones, making the soaked rice for the *sandnas* and *odes* to go with the meat dishes.

While all this bustling was going on, someone announced: "The author of the posters is caught!"

"Who?"

"Mario-Bab."

The chapel of the Holy Cross glittered with electric bulbs installed for the occasion. Nothing had ever looked so beautiful to the villagers. Dressed in their best, accompanied by their relatives, they were on their way to the chapel for Vespers. It was a time to be proud of the village. But on the way, many saw Regedor Flemingo dragging Mario like a sack of paddy and their festive spirit deadened.

The Committee of Inquiry was called together for an emergency session. Mario was brought in, and they looked at him as if they were ready to tear him to pieces and throw the bits to the vultures. But Mario met their hatred with a fierce look of honesty in his eyes.

"Are the posters your work, Mario?" rasped Regedor Flemingo.

"Yes, indeed, they are!" he answered. "Is the stealing of paddy from the *Casa de Comunidades* your work, senhor Regedor Flemingo Fonseca?"

For a moment the Committee of Inquiry was stunned.

"You aren't here to interrogate us with your lunatic questions. Do you understand that, Mario?" said Baltazar.

"Why not?" demanded Mario with equal passion.

Baltazar got up from his chair and slapped Mario hard. "You ought to know enough to respect authority and your elders!"

"You people do whatever you like with me, but you'll never stop me from thinking and the more I think, the more I know that you all are rotten hypocrites and thieves!"

"What idiocy are you talking?" asked Baltazar.

"Senhor Baltazar and Regedor Flemingo, did you or didn't you steal the paddy from the storeroom of the *Casa de Comunidades*?"

Again, silence descended, clouding two faces with guilt. Again, Baltazar was the first to regain his composure. "I've told you, Mario, you aren't here to interrogate us."

"This inquiry is a farce; you're holding it to save your own skins. Tar Menin, Petu-Bab and Mar Vicente aren't the thieves. You know who are the real thieves! You, senhor Baltazar, you are the thief! Regedor Flemingo, you are the thief!"

"Flog him! Flog him!" screeched Regedor Flemingo. "It isn't the son of Rosa who is speaking, it's that Devil in him."

"Flog him! Flog him!" Baltazar shouted.

But Mario went on, "Last year, Regedor Flemingo, you were the President of the *Fábrica*, and what did you do? You auctioned the lands of the *Fábrica* without informing the parishioners; and you and your cronies grabbed those lands for a song. You might have justified that to your conscience, if you have one; but how can you justify stealing the paddy, collected for taxes? You're nothing but a thief!"

"He's possessed! He's possessed!" the vicar and the chaplain shouted together.

"I'm ashamed! I'm ashamed!" cried Maximiano Jaques bitterly. "Why did the Devil choose my son?"

"Don't worry," the vicar consoled him, "I'll drive the Devil away from him."

Mario was stripped and flogged and the vicar sprinkled him with holy water, said a lot of prayers and in the name of God ordered the Devil to go to the depths of Hell.

Most of the villagers stayed to watch the inquiry and missed the fireworks display. Aquino Martins fumed.

The next day, the third of May, was the feast day of the Holy Cross. The previous day's incidents were left behind, and joviality blossomed once again in the village. The bell of the chapel rang and grenades boomed announcing that the time was approaching for the celebration of the mass. On the road, Aquino Martins and his three brothers, dressed in the *confraria* vestments, marched from his house to the beat of the drum to the chapel. On their heads were crowns of flowers, though only Aquino carried *vara*, with the dignity of a king.

The chapel was packed and crowds spilled onto the patio. The feira was full of happy customers; sellers were shouting their wares at the top of their voices. Then, suddenly, there was pandemonium, people running. The chapel emptied of the congregation much to the annoyance of the Four Brothers. Mario had been brought onto the patio. He was naked and his hands were bound behind him, his body showing the red marks of the flogging. They tied him to a coconut palm near the chapel and toddy was poured on his naked body to madden the tiger ants that were let loose on him. The hot summer sun beat viciously, but Mario, remaining immovable, bore the torture. In the eyes of the congregation, he was their beloved Saint Sebastião, who protected them from all diseases.

"Now," said one of the onlookers, "the ghost of José De Campos will surely leave Mario. He won't be able to bear this type of shame."

BOOK III

CHAPTER XIV

Time passed. In Goa, as in Portugal, and in her other colonies under the authoritarian regime of Prime Minister Salazar, the people had no rights of political expression. But when Dr. Manohar Lohia came to Goa on June 18th, 1946, at the invitation of his friend, Dr. Julião Menezes, opposition started to take shape. Lohia was a Socialist who had participated in India's freedom movement. During his brief stay in Goa, he and Julião Menezes started a civil rights movement. This campaign gathered momentum and the Colonial authorities, unused to any opposition, didn't know how to deal with it.

Mario was now seventeen years old, studying at the Institute of Abade Faria, Margão, the capital town of Salcete and an active centre for civil liberties.

One day, during this period, one of Mario's colleagues gave him a sheaf of *Portugal E Colonias*, a paper edited by Fanchu Loyola, an exile from Bombay. Though Fanchu Loyola was from Orlim, a village close to his, he didn't know who he was. Later on, he came to know that Fanchu was often persecuted by the Colonial Government for his political ideas and activism. Reading his articles and speeches, Mario could see clearly what was wrong with Goan society, and the measures that Fanchu proposed sounded right. Like him, Mario became convinced civil liberties were indispensable for any progress.

Goa had suddenly awakened; even in the villages the people gathered in big crowds to listen to speakers claiming their right to speak without fear. Some youths began wearing Indian-style clothes – homespun cloth and Gandhi caps – discarding the Western dress imposed upon them since the time of the Inquisition. On almost every wall of the main buildings in towns QUIT GOA was written, and QUIT GOA banners waved in the wind across the roads.

On the evening of the 20th of June, 1946, a large crowd gathered near the Dr. Jorge Barreto Square in Margão. Though it was the monsoon season, no rain came that day. The crowd was shouting defiance, laughing and catcalling at a police officer, Cabo Noronha, who stood aiming an old rusty cannon at them. Mario was in the crowd and for the first time he noticed that the people weren't timid any more.

"I'll shoot you! Disperse!" Cabo Noronha was shouting.

"Goans can't shoot Goans!" they teased him.

They all knew that though Cabo Noronha was given to drunken bouts of anger, he wouldn't have the courage to spill blood. Besides, the people suspected that the big gun was empty.

"Why have you gathered here?" a policeman asked.

"Don't you know?" responded the people.

"I don't. My orders are to break up the gathering."

"Tristão De Cunha is talking to us today."

"Who?"

"If you want to know, keep your mouth shut and listen."

"Tristão is an intellectual," Mario's classmate, Vishwanath Kamat, confided.

"I've never heard of him before," said Mario, embarrassed by his lack of knowledge.

"Most Goans haven't. He studied at the University of Sorbonne in Paris."

Mario wasn't impressed. Such foreign-educated Goans were usually the worst of the lot, totally assimilated and loyal to the Colonial Government.

"Tristão is different," said Vishwanath. "In Paris, he published articles explaining why India and Goa should be free from the colonial regimes. Tristão is well known in the intellectual circles of the West; he's a friend of the French philosopher Romain Rolland."

That hadn't impressed Mario either, but now he saw Tristão De Cunha standing before him. He was rather short, but undoubtedly an uncommon man among the common masses, an aristocrat wanting to spread his gospel among them. He was a man with a vision too. For some minutes, he held the audience with his eyes, and very awkwardly read a speech in Konkani. The crowd listened to him patiently, sometimes applauding. When Bertha Menezes, the daughter of Luis Menezes Bragança, spoke, it was in English. She also stressed the need for civil liberties. Ending her speech, she said, "If I can't talk in Konkani, it isn't my fault. It's the fault of the Colonialists."

Then the police dispersed the crowd, and as they ran helter-skelter, shouting JAI HIND! JAI GOA!, Mario was with them.

In June and July of 1946, Jorge Barreto Square became the Hyde Park Corner of Margão. The police couldn't stop the ardour of the people. They came to hear Bakibab Borkar, the well-known Goan poet, the speeches of Laxmikant Bhembre, Dr. Rama Hegde,

Purushotam Kakodkar, Fanchu Loyola and others. Though they differed in their approach, all of them had a vision of a free Goa; they gave what they had, never asking anything in return, and they influenced Mario immensely.

One day in July, he heard Evagrio Jorge speak. He found out that Evagrio was from Carmona, which surprised him, and that he was a pamphleteer who wrote in Konkani, rediscovering Goan history. Though his pamphlets were banned, Mario and many other youths read them and began to develop some pride in their past. Of all the speakers that Mario heard, Evagrio alone seemed to know the people, and the Konkani that he spoke was theirs.

"Once upon a time," he began with a soft lilt in his voice, and a strange, peaceful hush came over the audience, "There was a huge python. Every evening when the python went for a stroll, he passed an ant hill. The ants who got in his way were crushed. Every evening, ants died. They didn't know what to do. But they had to do something."

"What shall we do?" they asked.

"We must kill him," said one of them.

"He's so big and he's so strong! It's foolish to think that tiny ants like us can kill him."

"Nothing is foolish," said a wise ant. "Before we can teach him a lesson, we must stop thinking that we are too tiny and weak compared to the huge and powerful python. Our thoughts and actions should reflect our needs, and once we know our priorities, we should be one in our action, and then the huge and invincible python will be defeated."

The audience listened. The fable was making sense.

"But Goans can never unite!" some shouted.

"If we don't, that will be our doom," Evagrio said.

A hush fell over the audience.

"We shouldn't hold that thought," he continued. "Let me tell you what the ants did. If they stayed thinking they were small and weak, they wouldn't have achieved what they wanted. First, as I've told you, the habit of our thinking should be changed. That's very, very important. The ants in the fable did that." He paused and looked at the audience. "The ants marched and stood at both sides of the trail, waiting for the python, and when they saw him coming, they all bit him simultaneously with their tiny fangs. The python wriggled in agony, killing many ants. But that didn't scare them.

They were determined to achieve their end, and when the python
retreated in agony and never again used that trail, the ants shed their
belief in its invincibility. The mighty and the powerful can be taught
a lesson!"

It was late now, time to disperse. As Mario bicycled home on the
maroon dirt-road, many thoughts buzzed in his mind. He wasn't the
only one who had such ideas; there were many before him, and there
would be many more after him. Above, the sky was pregnant with
black monsoon clouds, about to open in a downpour, a good omen.
His heart was filled with hope.

But the Portuguese authorities had no intention of allowing their
power to erode in Goa or elsewhere in their colonies. Before the end
of June, Tristão De Cunha was arrested, and as the year went by,
Laxmikant Bhembre, Purushotam Kakodkar, Rama Hegde, Fanchu
Loyola were also arrested and then deported to Portugal and jailed
at Peniche Fort. Evagrio Jorge and others were imprisoned in the Fort
of Aguada.

CHAPTER XV

The imprisonment of their leaders did not deter the people. In the mornings, men and women marched in their towns, chanting for civil liberties. All the enraged Government could think of was to let loose its fury on the peaceful demonstrators. In one of the daily marches, Mario was near a girl who was being beaten by a police officer.

"You brute!" he yelled. "Take your hands off her!"

"Keep your mouth shut, you vermin! Or I'll pound you instead!"

"Why don't you?" he retorted. "It's cowardly to beat a girl!"

The police officer was abashed.

"Coward! Coward!" howled the other marchers.

Defiantly, Mario snatched the truncheon from the police officer, and looking into his eyes, said, "Go ahead, beat me!"

"Come along with me," the police officer snapped, grabbing back his truncheon and collaring Mario.

"Take me too! Take me too!" the girl went on shouting.

The police officer looked at her dismissively.

The girl followed them, and grabbing the officer's hand, she yelled, "Take me to the *Quartel*, you brute!" Though he was provoked, he controlled his anger; he didn't want to lift his hand against her again.

Mario was touched by her spirit, and when he looked at her, their eyes met. She was tall and slender, dressed in a blue sari, with her hair in a snake-like braid, slithering gracefully down her back. She was beautiful, he thought.

When at last the officer managed to get Mario to the police station, the girl wasn't allowed in, though she made a lot of noise. When she realised they were ignoring her, she cooled down and sat waiting on the steps for Mario to come out. The whole morning passed. It was afternoon before Mario appeared. She leapt to her feet and ran to him. Mario, who had never embraced a girl before, dropped all the restraints of his upbringing as she rushed into his arms.

"What did they do with you in there? Did they torture you?"

"No."

As they walked away from the police station, the girl held Mario's hand, but he pulled it way as gently as he could. There would be too many wagging tongues if this intimacy was seen. "Are you afraid to hold my hand?"

"No," he lied. "But I don't even know your name."

"Nirmala Karapurkar."

She held his hand again, and this time, he clasped hers.

"What did they do to you in there?"

"The Police Officer gave me a big lecture."

"Didn't he touch you at all?"

"No."

"I'm surprised. What did he say?"

"He said that the students should concentrate on their studies and not take part in useless demonstrations."

"What was your response?"

"I just listened."

"You just listened!" she snapped, and then in a calmer tone she said, "These idiots must be told that freedom of speech is the birthright of every individual. We of this generation have the duty to bring the colonial order down."

They walked. She asked him question after question, expressing her views fervently about all manner of things. Mario, swept away by her intelligence and beauty, didn't realise he had reached her house, until she tugged him down a side street before he had the chance to object.

"You must be hungry," she said. "I am. Let's go to my house."

It was a big house. Later Mario came to know that it was one of the wealthy *Saraswat brahmin* houses in Margão. Here, Nirmala's grandfather, an active eighty-year-old, ruled over the household of his sons, their wives and numerous children. He was a shrewd businessman who had built up the family wealth, trading in copra. Though he learnt to read and write Portuguese, and often spoke the language, he lived supported by the taboos and rituals of his caste and religion. He had the savvy to go along with all the sectors of the Goan population, and this had helped him to advance in his business. By economising, he gradually bought a mill and made better profits by extracting oil from copra, unhusking paddy and making flour. Because buying an estate meant status and a good investment, he bought one from a Catholic landlord who was going bankrupt. Now he had the itch to gain influence in the Colonial administration. He wanted the best of the two words for his three sons: the best from Hinduism and the best from the Portuguese; the two could coexist without contaminating his Hindu soul. He wore a Western jacket and tie, a black cap on his head, covered his legs with dhoti and wore sandals. But whatever his outward appearance, he was a Saraswat brahmin at heart.

"Come in," called Nirmala, as she bounced up the steps to her house, taking off her sandals before crossing the threshold.

Mario followed suit. He had always got along well with Hindu boys from his village, and their mothers often offered him food on banana leaves or on *potraoir*. These weren't like Nirmala's family; they were poor Hindus, mostly of the goldsmith caste, who lived on the lands of the Catholic landlords. Nirmala's father, Xembu Karapurkar, had studied in the universities of Portugal, qualifying as an advocate, a very successful and popular one. One brother was *escrivão de Comunidades*, a Government official, and the other managed the business that their father had established.

"Make yourself at home," said Nirmala, then she disappeared somewhere in the house.

The living room was quite modest. But it was very tidy with a few chairs and a sofa, and its cement floor was spotless and shining. Mario made himself comfortable in a chair. There were no portraits of family ancestors hanging here; instead there were a few framed scenes from the *Ramayana* and a framed picture of Lord Krishna playing on the flute. Somewhere in the house incense sticks burned. Something in all this spoke to him, and he felt something submerged within him rising to the surface. As he looked at the pictures he wanted to know what they meant. Yes, he had to find out about his old culture, the culture before the conquest of Goa. He had been robbed of that, and now he didn't belong either to the Iberian culture or to the culture of his pre-conquest ancestors. He was just a *canarim*.

"Would you like to have a glass of water?"

Mario shifted his gaze from the pictures and looked at the woman standing before him. She held out a glass of water and a lump of sugar. He knew at once that she was Nirmala's *aii*, her mother. He smiled shyly.

"Thank you," he said, almost inaudibly.

As Mario chewed the lump of sugar and drank the cool water, he felt embarrassed. Nirmala's mother, still standing there, was looking at him minutely. He felt he should say something, but didn't know what. She looked very young, her hair parted in the middle and held together at the back in the shape of a bun. On her forehead was a red dot, on her neck, a chain of tiny black beads, both symbols of her marriage. His eyes met hers and he felt that she looked at him with mistrust.

"Hi, Mario," called Nirmala coming into the living room. She introduced him to her mother, "Aii, this is Mario."

Nirmala's mother folded her hands in greeting Mario, but there was no smile on her face. Mario returned the greeting by holding his hands.

"Aii, do you know how Mario defied the police today?"

"No," she snapped, and casting an angry look at Nirmala, she left.

Mario felt he wasn't welcome here; he was a village Catholic boy in a high-caste Hindu home.

"I must leave," he said, getting up.

"Why? Eat and leave. I've already prepared some food for you. Are you offended by my mother's reaction?"

Mario didn't answer.

"Don't be sensitive," she said. "I know you're a Christian and I'm a Hindu. Your parents are bound to their customs and my parents to ours. But it's our generation's duty to break the grip of all that divides us."

"It is."

"Before everything else, we're all humans," said Nirmala. "We should be liberated from prejudices; it's only then that the society won't be prey to whatever hate campaign that some fanatical leaders might stir up."

"You're right, Nirmala. Goa won't be truly liberated unless there is self-liberation for each Goan. Otherwise..."

"Otherwise what, Mario?"

"As you have said, Nirmala, the religious fanatics, zealous caste supremacists, profiteers and those hungry for power will exploit the people to their advantage."

Mario was enthralled that Nirmala's views so coincided with his.

"I'm glad to have had this conversation with you," he said sincerely and left.

CHAPTER XVI

Mario didn't go home straight away. He wanted to be alone, so he biked along the red dirt road to the Monte, a hill in Margão. When he reached his favourite spot, he sat, his back against the trunk of a cashew tree, his legs spread on the ground.

The sun was mild. In the bushes bulbuls sang, and far off on a tall tree, he heard a dove cooing. Beyond, a luminous blood-red sun was sinking into the Arabian Sea. Mario closed his eyes and in the hush he heard a continuous rhythmic sound, the breathing of the earth. Then that too ceased, and as the external world began to close itself off from him, he journeyed deeper and deeper within. There was Nirmala, erect and elegant, waiting for him, a smile shimmering on her face. Enchanted, he looked at her; she was peaceful and serene. But when his eyes went to her cashew-apple bosoms pointing through her blouse, his blood rose. He struggled to push away feelings of desire, but they rushed in with greater force. No, he didn't want to yield to such pleasures yet. He struggled and struggled and in the end, the storm subsided.

Though he would have liked to stay in this world, he was tugged back to the humdrum world of men. The sun had long gone, and the birds lay quiet on their perches, though he saw an erratic crow hurrying to its perch. He mounted his bike to go home and as he sped down the slope, a soothing joy breezed within him.

Arriving home, he saw his father on the veranda as usual, talking to senhor Tolentinho, Dr. Maurice and the chaplain. Seeing Mario entering the house, his father called, "Go and put your bike in its place and then come here, Mario. I want to talk to you."

Mario hadn't been close to his father for years, though he loved him. Maximiano, who had hoped that Mario would outgrow his childish pranks, was pained that his son was a radical. That night, because the Goan dailies had reported the landing of Portuguese troops in Goa, and teacher Marcos had spoken about the earlier struggles against the Portuguese and the original conquest, the implications of his son's involvement in the protest marches caused him alarm. Teacher Marcos' intense accounts brought alive disturb-

ing images of the past. He heard the cries of the tortured Goans and
the screams of the women as they were raped by the conquistadors.
Before his eyes, he saw the severed heads of Goan rebels paraded on
top of long bamboo pikes; defiant Goans dragged behind horses;
thousands of Goans set on fire. The elders' warnings never to arouse
the ire of the *firngo* sprang up in his mind. They had told him that like
God who had cast the rebellious Lucifer and his fallen angels into
Hell, the Portuguese conquistadors had tortured and butchered
Goans and thrown them into the depths of wells. He had learned
obedience to such terrors, but what about Mario, his son?

As a father he had tried his best to pass on his colonial inheritance, but Mario hadn't taken it. Did he hear the voices of his
ancestors asking for vengeance? But why should one become involved in the injustices of the past? What mattered was the present.
And, at present, the Almighty Salazar sat enthroned as the head of
the Portuguese empire. Why should one give cause to arouse his
wrath?

"Papa," said Mario who had now returned. He greeted the other
notables who were there.

Maximiano loved his son, and all he wanted was that no harm
should come to him. Maximiano handed him *Vida*, a Portuguese
daily, and Mario read about the landing of the overseas Portuguese
troops.

"What do you say now, Mario?" asked Teacher Marcos.

Mario said nothing.

"No more protest marches for you," joked senhor Tolentinho.

"Can anyone blame Dr. Salazar for sending troops to Goa?" the
chaplain asked. "No respectable father can put up with the
disobedience of his children. Impertinent children must be pun-
ished for their own good."

"Look, Mario," said Maximiano, anxious to impress his companions. "You are my only son. I love you and always will. I raised you
and did my best to instil in you respect for authority. I didn't spare
the cane on you, and did what I could to bring you to your books.
Mario, you failed me, I didn't fail you."

He understood his father's concern.

"You people don't know anything about Portuguese history,"
said Teacher Marcos. "Portugal will return love for love, but if you
disturb their order, then you have had it. With the largeness of their

hearts, they took pride in *lusitanising* us, but why do we pay them with ingratitude? Who can blame the Portuguese if they let loose terror on unworthy Goans? People like T.B. Cunha, Evagrio Jorge, Purshotam Kakodkar, Dr. Rama Hegde, Fanchu Loyola and others like them will make Goans pay hell!"

"Politics isn't for the common man," said senhor Tolentinho. "It's ok for T. B. Cunha. He's a rich landlord and a bachelor. What else can he do? Indulge in politics! He can afford it, but not you. Keep away from it! That's my advice. See Evagrio Jorge from Carmona, the only son of his widowed mother, languishing in jail and for what? He doesn't see his mother's tears. Don't waste yourself in a jail, Mario."

"Listen to senhor Tolentinho, Mario," Maximiano pleaded.

The notables left to go home and Rosa lit the oil lamp in the oratorio. She called her husband and her son to come for the rosary. When the rosary was over, Mario with his hands folded, went first to his father and then to his mother to get their blessings. But his father was still deep in prayer, asking the saints over and over again where he had failed as a father. Tears rolled down his cheeks and Mario was touched, but he couldn't give up his dreams. Maximiano sighed and looked at Mario. He lifted his right hand, but before blessing him said, "Promise me that you'll keep away from politics. You heard what senhor Tolentinho and the others said."

Mario didn't reply, but Maximiano still blessed his son.

Rosa, too, was afraid for Mario. She knew why the Portuguese troops were in Goa, and hadn't forgotten that he was the gift of the Holy Cross. Her old fears returned as she saw Mario before her with his hands folded, waiting to be blessed. She wanted to see a beautiful girl in his arms and not that flat wooden Cross. There should be a daughter-in-law devouring him with her kisses, and not that Cross taking pleasure in his pain. Her daughter-in-law would give Mario the pleasures of the flesh, she would be a grandmother and the ancestral house would be filled with the noises of Mario's children. What a joy it would be to look after them! Then she would have no regrets when God called her. She even imagined herself in her coffin, surrounded by her husband, her son and her daughter-in-law. She saw her husband choked with grief, Mario sobbing like a child, holding his youngest, a daughter, named after her, and her daughter-in-law crying the roof off with mournful dirges. What a beautiful death! The Cross would rob her of that.

"Mother!" said Mario. Rosa was startled back to reality. She blessed her son.

Many thoughts crowded Mario's brain as he lay on his bed that night. When sleep overtook him, he began to dream, not of paradise but of Nirmala. She stood before him naked, elegant and enchantingly beautiful. Her hair, no longer in a twisted braid, cascaded down her back and her smile was shy, but her eyes shone with desire. When Mario set his eyes on her long slender legs and on the cleft patch of hair between them, the blood within him rose. He shed his clothes and stood naked before her. He took her in his arms, desire exploding. He wanted to be joined with her – one being, one soul.

CHAPTER XVII

One morning, shrieks rang out from the house of Jozin-Bab, the centenarian of Cavelossim. His daughter-in-law, Maroz, who had gone to awaken him for his breakfast, found him dead. Other members of the household and the neighbours came running.

"Did he receive the last sacrament?" asked Neunita.

"No, he didn't," sobbed Antonio, Jozin-Bab's only son. "But he made a good confession and only yesterday morning, the chaplain gave him Holy Communion."

Neunita at once took out her beads and started the rosary. She prayed loudly, uttering each word of the prayer solemnly. She ordered Antonio, who was wailing, "*Pai gha! Pai gha!*" to say a decade to his father's soul. "It will do a lot more good for his soul than your wailing," she admonished.

When the rosary was over, the village elders helped Antonio draw up plans for the funeral. Jozin-Bab's body was washed and dressed. Cursin, the village jack-of-all trades, came forward to do this; only he was bold enough for such jobs. Oji-mai Concentin was courageous too, but she dressed only dead females. Because Jozin-Bab was a member of the chaddo brotherhood, Santana Martins, a chaddo to the bone, insisted that Jozin-Bab had the right to wear his *confraria* vestments even in his death. The other chaddo men knew that in doing so, they were defying the ecclesiastical authorities and Antonio was strongly against it. Don José da Costa Nunes, the Portuguese Bishop of Goa had passed an ordinance amalgamating all the confrarias into one. The higher castes had resisted this, so the Patriarch had banned them from wearing their vestments at any ceremonies. But on Santana Martins' orders, Cursin dressed Jozin-Bab with the white *muça* and the red *opa*, the chaddo confraria vestments.

Then Jozin-Bab was laid on a mat, his head resting on a white pillow. His hands were clasped together, his rosary beads entwined around them. In the candleholders near his head long tapers burned; at his back was placed a huge crucifix from the family chapel of Baltazar Afonso. Couriers were sent to his distant relatives to inform them of his death. The bells of the chapel and of the church tolled sorrowfully every half-hour. His relatives and the villagers came in droves to pay him their last respects.

The villagers brought vegetables and poultry, and the fishermen brought fish to Antonio's house. Toddy tapper Inas donated a *feni codso*, and others gave their labour free; they all respected Jozin-Bab. They had thought that he would never die and his death shocked them as much as the untimely passing of someone much younger. It was lucky that Antonio's wife, Maroz, hadn't sold the pig she'd been raising. She had raised pigs for years with the intention of slaughtering them for Jozin-Bab's funeral banquet, but God seemed to have forgotten him, so the pigs were always eventually sold. Petu-Bab, Tar Menin, Cursin and Hut João chased this one all over the village and finally they caught it. Petu-Bab cut a hole in its throat.

"Bring in the container for the blood," cried Cursin, while the pig shrieked as its life poured out. Mazancit, the village chef, came running with a *cune* to put the blood in.

"It's red and thick," she said. "It'll make nice sorpartel."

"Don't forget to give us big portions," Hut João told Mazancit. "I haven't had sorpartel for ages."

"No weddings, no funerals means no sorpartel," joked Tar Menin. "Mazancit, you'd better make this a very good sorpartel, if not Jozin-Bab will give you hell wherever he is gone."

Mazancit smiled as she picked up the blood and went back to the kitchen. The butchers made palm torches and burnt the pig's bristles, and then scraped its skin with sharp pieces of tiles, until the carcass was clean and ivory white.

"The pig looks like a *paclo* now," said Amalia Barros, Tar Menins's sixteen year old niece. The only white man that she had seen – before the troops came – was the Patriarch of Goa when he'd come to Carmona to confirm some new communicants, she being one of them. As he had traced the cross on her forehead, she had looked at the Patriarch minutely. He did look different from the other men around her. Was he really God? Perhaps in Heaven all people must be white like him. If she died a good girl, would she go to Heaven and be white? What joy! But then someone had told her that he came from Portugal. Was this place in Heaven? Recently, though, she had seen the white troops stationed in Goa going up and down the roads in the military jeeps and lorries. She also saw the black troops. Were they devils? She was confused.

"It's a good comparison," said Cursin. "The paclo's skin indeed looks like the carcass of this pig."

"You shut up there!" Tar Menin snarled.

"But she has sharp eyes, hasn't she?"

"I've told you to shut up," said Tar Menin, and turning to Amalia, he warned, "You, girl, don't talk about paclo here or anywhere else."

"Why?" she demanded.

Tar Menin looked at Amalia. She was budding into womanhood and he was afraid of what the sex-starved Portuguese soldiers might do to their women folk. He had to talk some sense into the girl. "They are like a swarm of grasshoppers who come to devour the rice-seedlings," he said.

"That can't be true," she said. "They are here to protect us."

"Protect us from what?"

"I don't know; but the chaplain said that they are like angels sent from Heaven to protect us from devils."

"Devils?" Hut João was curious. "What devils?"

"Like Mario-Bab, your godson. Chaplain says that Mario-Bab doesn't believe in God and he's a Communist."

"What's a Communist?" asked Cursin.

"Communists don't believe in God, they tread on the sacred image of Jesus, they demolish churches, they respect no authority and they do a lot more bad things," Amalia enlightened them.

Hut João was angry. Who knew Mario better than he? If Mario was a Communist, as Amalia said, how could he be so kind and generous? True, Mario did a lot of foolish things, but that didn't make him a Communist. Who had taught him, João, to read and write, and many others too? With his godson's help, he had read parts of the New Testament in Konkani and that had opened his mind. And when his godson told him that he wasn't inferior to his landlord before God, it had made him think.

"He isn't a Communist," growled Hut João. "He loves us, the poor people. You're wrong, Amalia."

But before Amalia could open her mouth, Cursin, in all serious-ness, asked, "Are Portuguese men's pricks white or black?"

Amalia ran away blushing and Tar Menin scolded Cursin.

Jozin-Bab's house was full beyond capacity as people poured in from far and near. As each group heard the dirges coming from the house, they began wailing, and the cries reached a pitch of sorrow as

the coffin arrived and Jozin-Bab was laid in it. So many people to
share his last meal and so many people praying for his soul! Rosa was
there with Mario, and she remembered what Jozin-Bab had said
about her son. He had told her that he was a seed sown among thorny
bushes and when he grew up, he would be chopped down by a
woodcutter. Was this prophecy going to be fulfilled with the arrival
of Portuguese troops? She looked at Jozin-Bab in his coffin and
prayed for his spirit to intercede on Mario's behalf.

It was night now. The mourners had drained all their grief and
sat exhausted and quiet. Jozin-Bab's face was serene in the glow of
the candles, and Mario looking at him wondered why men spent all
their energies in fighting and quarrelling. As such thoughts ran
through his mind, a commotion disturbed the silence.

"The *pacles* are here!" someone called in panic.

When Mario came out he saw a jeep parked near Jozin-Bab's
porch, its headlights still on. Seeing that no one else had the courage
to approach them, he stepped forward and asked, "What's wrong?"

They handed him a piece of paper. Rosa looked terrified,
thinking they must have come for her son. When it became clear that
he wasn't their target, she relaxed and even began to feel proud of
the way her son was conducting himself. He hadn't stayed tongue-
tied like the others, but as an equal he had asked them what they
had come for, talking to them in their own tongue.

Mario explained to Antonio that the paper was a decree forbid-
ding Jozin-Bab's interment in the vestments of the chaddo confraria.
Stammering in terror, Antonio made Mario tell the military police
that he had nothing to do with dressing his father.

"If it wasn't you, who did it?" they wanted to know.

"It was Santana Martins!" he said, and felt sick at this betrayal.

Santana Martins was called. It was said that at the height of the
caste conflicts, he had fired shots at the Patriarch when he had come
to Cavellosim on a pastoral visit. But because there wasn't sufficient
proof, he hadn't been arrested, though the Patriarch had excommu-
nicated him.

"It's our right," he told the military police, "and no law can take
it away from us."

They looked at him sternly. Before they could say anything,
Mario asked, "Who told you that the deceased was dressed in the
confraria vestments?"

"That's none of your business."

But it wasn't difficult to guess who must have lodged the complaint at the Quartel. Since the passing of that ecclesiastical law, the sudras had been hankering for admission into the confrarias of the upper castes. They too wanted to wear upper caste vestments and celebrate the feasts of the patron saints of the upper castes. Then their sons and daughters would marry into the higher castes. This, of course, worried the upper castes. They would rather have had the confrarias dissolved than give the sudras a chance to get their foot in. Let them in and they would behave like camels in a tent! Now the sudras of Cavelossim and Carmona were clamouring to be Jozin-Bab's pallbearers. Such an honour would be a step nearer to acceptance in upper caste circles, but the chaddos of Cavelossim wouldn't budge.

Mario didn't know how to solve the problem. He could see the impatience on the faces of the white police. One of them said, "I thought the Goans were nationalists who wanted to get rid of Portuguese rule. But what I see here are just caste supremacists. You are people who mix up religion with all sorts of superstitions. God knows how many loyalties you have!"

"That's indeed what Goans are," Mario agreed.

Then the chaplain arrived as if he had come for a leisurely stroll, and behind him came the parish choirboys in their gowns and surplices, each holding a candle-holder with a lit taper. One carried a small portable stoup and a sprinkler and another rang a small bell – tim... tim... tim... a monotonous, sad sound. Maroz heard it and, being a good daughter-in-law, she bawled, "*Pai gha! Pai gha!* Don't go, *Pai*, don't leave us *Pai. Pai! Pai!*"

"Calm down, Maroz, calm down," the other women begged, though they admired the quality of her grief.

The chaplain intoned loudly the *Sign of the Cross*, dipped the sprinkler in the stoup and rained holy water on Jozin-Bab, and at this signal, Vicente Mestri, the parish teacher started a Latin chant, loud and clear.

Though the funeral rites had started, no solution had been found for the dispute. Santana Martins was adamant that Jozin-Bab should be buried in his confraria vestments and that the chaddo irmãos should be allowed to wear their vestments in the funeral procession. The military police threatened Santana Martins that they would be jailed.

"It's already six," a mourner said, "if we don't bury Jozin-Bab soon, he'll start decomposing."

Mario was exasperated with his people's pettiness. In desperation he asked the military police, "If the sudra and the chaddo come to an accord, would you allow the burial to proceed?"

The military police, instructed by their superiors to handle the situation sensitively, were only too ready to agree.

All around Mario were the people he had known since he was a child. If they couldn't resolve their differences, poor Jozin-Bab wouldn't be buried. He waited until total silence had fallen.

"My brothers and sisters, we haven't come here to fight over caste values, have we?"

"No," he heard someone say.

"Why have we come here?"

"To bury Jozin-Bab, of course."

"Can anyone here tell me what caste God belongs to?" He waited for the answer but no one responded.

"Is God a chaddo, senhor Martins?"

All eyes were on Santana Martins and he was embarrassed. He didn't answer.

Now Mario looked at Evaristo Afonso, the leader of Cavelossim's sudras; it was he who had lodged the complaint. "Is God a sudra, senhor Evaristo Afonso?"

Evaristo, confused, lowered his head without making any comment.

Mario looked at the people again. He saw Hut João, Tar Menin, Mud Bosteão, Oji-mai, Cursin, Modo-mai, Mar Anton – all those nonpersons, and he saw their eyes glistening. His heart was filled with love.

"God is not a brahmin, God is not a chaddo, and God is not a sudra. Isn't that so, chaplain?"

The chaplain looked at Mario, but didn't answer.

Though the military police couldn't understand Konkani, they knew that something was happening. They realised that Mario had potential as a leader, and though he was being helpful at this time, they would have to watch him.

"Let me tell you what God is," Mario said. "God is love and nothing else."

No one contradicted what Mario said. He spoke again, "I know that there is love in your hearts, and that means God is in your hearts.

And because there is love in you, and because there is God in you, we will bury Jozin-Bab with the love and respect that he deserves. Is there anyone among you who would take this honour from him?"

Heads shook in denial.

"Why shouldn't the pallbearers of Jozin-Bab come from both the confrarias?" Mario asked.

Even Santana Martins had no heart to object, and though Evaristo wanted to protest, he knew that village opinion would be firmly against him.

No one was buried in that village with more dignity and honour than Jozin-Bab. The members of both the confrarias, the chaddos donning their white opa and red muça, and the sudras with opa and blue muça, both carrying lit tapers, marched in two parallel rows, and the choirboys following them sang *Our Father* in sorrowful, monotonous tones. The pallbearers, three from the sudra confraria and three from the chaddo confraria carried the coffin with solemn dignity and Anaclet's band, following the procession, played funeral marches. At the back, Antonio, supported by his friends, grief-stricken, barefoot and dishevelled, a white handkerchief around his neck, cried, *Pai gha! Pai gha!*

After the burial, teacher Marcos gave the funeral eulogy. Ending it, he raised his eyes to the sky and said, "Villagers, I see the happy spirit of Jozin-Bab climbing the heavenly ladder, and before we reach home, Jozin-Bab will be in Heaven."

CHAPTER XVIII

Mario's reputation amongst the poorest villagers was very high. His handling of the dispute at the funeral house had impressed many, but among the leaders of both the chaddos and the sudras, he had made enemies. He had come to destroy the fabric of their society, which had survived as a piece from generation to generation in spite of Christianity and Colonialism. The elite sudras didn't want a caste-less society: they wanted acceptance into the higher castes.

"Is it true that the centenarian of your village wouldn't have been buried but for you?" Nirmala asked Mario when she met him in Margão, the next day.

"Who told you?"

"News travels fast, Mario," she said, holding his hand and squeezing it with love. "I'm proud of you, Mario."

"Come," he said to her lovingly, "Let us go to the Monte."

As they walked, neither of them spoke. They had boundaries to cross; she was a Hindu Saraswat brahmin and he a chaddo Christian. A Catholic marry a Hindu? Sacrilege! A brahmin woman marry a Catholic man? Pollution! Not all the water of the Ganges would wash her clean. But as they sat under a cashew bush on the Monte, none of this meant anything to them.

They talked in whispers in each others' arms, their hearts beating faster, the blood racing in their veins. Mario tried to kiss her; she was shy, but he held her tight; then she returned his passion and sought his lips, again and again.

But before it was over, an angry shout disturbed them.

Before them stood Madeu Karapurkar, Nirmala's cousin. Nirmala's mother, fearing that her daughter was getting involved with a Catholic boy, had asked Madeu to spy on her. Madeu and Nirmala were old rivals. Madeu understood that money was happiness, and that as long as the colonial regime lasted, the business class would continue to amass wealth.

"You want freedom?" he would ask Nirmala.

"Of course."

"What's freedom without money?"

"When Goa is free," Nirmala would argue, "Goan businessmen will have a better opportunity to make money."

"Nonsense," Madeu would say, "the big magnates from India will swamp Goa with their capital. And where will the Goan businessmen be? We'll be paupers in our own land."

"That isn't true," Nirmala would object. "In free Goa, Goans will legislate. They'll make the laws and they'll control Goa's economy."

"It doesn't happen that way. The one who has the capital rules. The Goan economy will come into the hands of Indian capitalists."

Madeu would dismiss her as a mere woman, with foolish ideas; in the end, she would have a husband and children and that would be it. Nirmala hated the way he patronised her.

"How dare you spy on me!" she raged.

He ignored her contemptuously and, fixing a look of hatred on Mario, he screamed, "How dare you lay your filthy hands on a Hindu girl! You pork-eating son of a Catholic bitch!"

Mario ignored this outburst.

"You have the nerve to seduce a Hindu girl! You filthy pig!"

"He didn't seduce me," Nirmala shouted.

"You shut your mouth," Madeu yelled back at her. "You're a slut! Running after a Christian boy!"

"You're an idiot, Madeu! And always have been!"

"I'll show you who is an idiot, when I get you home."

"As if I care!"

A surge of loathing rose in Madeu and he sprang like a disturbed lion, slapping Mario with all his strength, drawing blood from his mouth. Though Mario was angry, he didn't strike back.

"Who do you think you are!" said Madeu, "Another Gandhi?"

When Mario said nothing, Madeu didn't raise his hand again, but warned, "If I see you again with Nirmala, I'll kill you. You understand that, pig?"

"He isn't a pig," Nirmala protested. "Pigs are like you, Madeu. You had no right to slap him."

"You're coming with me now!" Madeu bellowed, and grabbed Nirmala's wrist. "Your mother asked me to keep an eye on you. For her sake and our family's honour, you must come."

At home, Madeu reported to Nirmala's mother what he had seen. She said nothing to her daughter; it was too serious a matter to bandy words with her. This would have to be dealt with by the family council, presided over by Nirmala's grandfather.

When the grandfather was informed of Nirmala's doings, he was shocked, but being a practical man, he remained calm. At 8.00 p.m. the next day, Nirmala's uncles, father and grandfather assembled to hear the case. The only women in this assembly were Nirmala and her mother, who was the complainant.

"Is it true, what Madeu has reported about you?" asked Vitol Karapurkar, starting the proceedings.

"What did he tell you, grandfather?" Nirmala asked defiantly.

Eyebrows were raised. This wasn't the submissiveness required of a girl. Vitol Karapurkar, though, didn't loose his temper; it would require patience to bring this headstrong girl back into the fold. To do this was his duty to his family, their caste and their religion. Hundreds of years ago, the Hindus of Goa had resisted conversion to Christianity in spite of Portuguese brutality, so he wasn't going to allow Nirmala to slip willingly into the arms of a Catholic boy. The very idea enraged him, but he knew Nirmala too well to risk showing what he really felt. She would only get more defiant and might even run away and expose their shame for all to see. But Nirmala's father couldn't restrain his anger and Nirmala's mother, shaking as if she had an earthquake inside her, cried hysterically, "I'll burn myself alive if I ever see you with that Christian boy!"

Nirmala knew that this wasn't an empty threat; her mother was a proud woman and would hold herself responsible for the shame her daughter was bringing on the family. Nirmala had no heart to hurt her mother, or any member of the family, bigots though they were. The defiance broke inside her.

"Nirmala," Vitol Karapurkar said gently.

"Yes, grandfather," she said almost inaudibly.

"You will not see that Christian boy again. Is that clear to you, Nirmala?"

Nirmala looked at the faces around her; she was their precious possession; she didn't belong to herself and despite her progressive attitudes, she could not bring herself to break from her family.

"Speak up, Nirmala," said her father.

"If that's what you want."

"That's our verdict and you must abide by it," Vitol Karapurkar declared.

"Very well," said Nirmala, defeated.

"One thing more. Politics isn't for women. Do you understand that?"

She bowed her head.

"The firnges and kapris the Portuguese brought here are already raping our women. You mustn't expose yourself to their whims. No member of this family will participate in politics. If the Portuguese regime collapses in Goa, it will do so when its time comes. We are businessmen and politics isn't for us."

Vitol Karapurcar dismissed the assembly, but ordered Pandurang and Shanti to stay behind. It was time for Nirmala to get married; that would put an end to her rebelliousness. Pandurang had, in fact, a boy in mind, though he had delayed advancing the marriage, because he wanted Nirmala to complete her education first – in these changing times it would make her a more desirable wife. The young man, Purshotam Raiturkar, was a Saraswat brahmin, from a wealthy legal family. He was studying to become a physician not in the *Escola Medica* in Panjim but in Bombay; later, he would go to England for further training. For their part, the young man's parents had also begun to feel marriage was urgent; they had heard so many stories about Hindu boys who had gone to England and returned with English wives.

"That's excellent. A perfect choice," said Vitol Karapurkar.

"So you approve?" asked Pandurang.

"I do. In fact, Purshotam's grandfather was a good friend of mine; he would be happy if he were alive to know his grandson was marrying my granddaughter."

"Well, then," said Pandurang. "It would be wise to call upon the Raiturkar family and propose the marriage. The boy is in his final year of medicine and will be coming home this month."

"Leave that to me," said Vitol Karapurkar.

But while her elders went to bed contented, Nirmala couldn't sleep. The whole night she tossed on her bed thinking that she wasn't what she'd thought herself to be; she only blabbered ideas that appealed to her, but she couldn't act on them. She couldn't live this way, she had to be true to her love and true to her ideas. Mario meant a lot to her; she had to be with him. There had to be a way.

CHAPTER XIX

Days went by and Mario heard nothing from Nirmala. He walked up and down the road by her house; even a glimpse of her would have been enough to calm him. Where were they hiding her? He went and knocked on her door, but no one answered. What must she be going through? He couldn't sleep, thinking about her. In his dreams, he would see her, beautiful and loving, but when he woke up, his depression returned. One day, though, the postman brought him a letter. His hands trembling, he opened it and read:

Dearest Mario,

Ages have gone by and I haven't seen you. I long to be in your arms. I dream about you. If I didn't dream about you, I would have gone crazy. It is in dreams that you hold me, it is in dreams that you caress me, it is in dreams that I kiss you and then the pain subsides. I can't bear this separation.

Something I must confess. I'm not as strong willed as I thought myself to be. Though I can't agree with my elders, yet I can't get away from their grip. I can't bear to hurt them. What am I supposed to do? I'm confused.

I'm shut in a room and under the constant vigilance of Madeu and other cousins. It was sheer good luck that I was able to smuggle this letter out. I feel your despair, but what can I do? If I get another opportunity like this one, I'll write again. Also, let me warn you that my elders are planning to give me in marriage. I'll never betray the love that I have for you.

I love you and always will,
Nirmala.

He read the letter again and again and his longing for her was so acute that he wished that his flesh could melt and he become a spirit and go to her. Days passed, weeks went by, and no further letter came. He walked by her house but didn't see her. He lost his zest for life. Rosa couldn't miss the signs.

"Mario," she said affectionately, "what's the matter?"

"Nothing."

"I'm your mother. Share your troubles with me."

Mario looked at her. Would she understand? She was a devoted Catholic. Could she approve of his love for a Hindu girl?

"Are you in political trouble?"

"No."

"Then, what's wrong?"

"I'm in love," he said shyly.

Rosa couldn't believe it. Her son in love! The dark monsoon clouds of her fearful dream receded. Perhaps, after all, the Holy Cross wasn't going to be Mario's bride. Her son had the same desires as any other man, to marry and have a family. Happy visions blossomed. Now for sure, she would be a grandmother. Tears of joy brimmed in her eyes.

"Who's the girl?"

"Nirmala."

"Nirmala?" she paused. There wasn't a saint in the Catholic calendar named Nirmala. "Nirmala, who?"

"Nirmala Karapurkar."

It was a Hindu name. She was not only a Hindu but a Hindu Saraswat brahmin. Nirmala was just an illusion, and the Cross was still saying, "I'm his chosen bride. No woman will have him."

Rosa, heaving with sorrow, embraced her son. How long was it since Mario had last cried in her arms and she had lulled him to sleep? It only seemed like yesterday to her.

"Mother," he said, "I love her so much. But..."

"Everything will be all right," she comforted him, but she knew she was lying. But then she began to think that it didn't matter if Nirmala was a Hindu. What she cared about most was that her son should take a bride of flesh and blood, for otherwise, who would know that once she, the wife of Maximiano Jaques, had born a son, and at his birth the rain had come and a terrible drought had been averted? No, she preferred Nirmala to the Cross.

"Is Nirmala beautiful?"

"Very."

"I wish I could see her."

"If you see her, you'll love her, Mother, even though, she isn't..."

There was a glimmer in her eyes, and Mario, noticing it, felt that his mother was relenting.

"Will my father approve?"

"Your father won't."

"And you...?"

"Well, you're my son."

But months went by and Mario didn't hear from Nirmala again. When the pain grew too great, he would come to his mother and she would try to console him.

One day, Tar Menin came with the news that Inez Teixeira, the daughter of a local fisherman from Cavelossim, had been raped by white soldiers. The whole village was shocked and angry. For a time, Mario's attention was held by this affair.

Inez was scarcely eighteen years old, in the bloom of her youth. Her copper coloured skin had a beautiful sheen and her teeth, ivory white, dazzled when she smiled. Her breasts stretched her blouse to the point of bursting and when she walked in a hurry, with a fish basket on her head, her behind swayed seductively. But though many men tried to trap her, she wouldn't take their bait. She would dismiss their advances firmly, but leave them with a smile. Though rebuffed, they weren't offended. Her ways won the hearts of all the villagers. Even the wives of the village notables liked her, not only because she ignored the amorous advances of their husbands, but because she would sell them the best fish.

"She was coming home all alone," Tar Menin said, and they were all ears for his story.

"Coming from where?"

"She was coming from Margão, after selling her fish, and as I said she was all alone. Her empty basket was on her head and as she walked, she munched roasted peanuts from a paper cone."

"That's what happens," one listener interrupted. "As soon as they get a catch, they rush to Margão, without selling to us villagers, and now see what has happened."

Tar Menin, without making any comment, resumed the story. "As she reached Jacniband, she felt very alone. There was only one other woman a long way in front of her and she felt uneasy. One never knows who hides in that dense cactus bush. She quickened her pace and ventured to look back. Then she noticed a military truck coming up behind her. She quickly stepped off the road; you know how dangerously they drive."

"They are like wild animals."

"Then?"

"Well, as I was telling you, they came with such speed and braked before her with such a screech. Poor girl! She almost died with fright!"

"Why didn't the woman ahead of her call for help?"

"What can you expect? She was afraid for herself. What if they ran after her?"

That made sense.

"Go on."

"Then they pounced upon her, caught hold of her and put her into their truck. Though she was paralysed with fear, she realised what was happening to her."

"Poor Inez!" remarked one woman. "Why can't St. Francis Xavier strike them with lightning?"

"He wouldn't do that."

"Why not?"

"St. Francis is a firngo; don't forget that."

"She fainted," Tar Menin went on, "but what did they care? They are the sort of people who..."

"I know what you mean!... They will do it even with a female corpse. That's what they are! How horrible!"

"There were five soldiers in the truck, and all of them, one after the other, mounted her."

"All of them?"

"All of them."

There was silence, but in the minds of the audience many thoughts throbbed. A beautiful woman like Inez raped, and raped by the whites; they couldn't take it; it wounded them.

"Beasts!"

"Of course they are beasts," said Tar Menin. "And when they had done their job, they tossed her out naked; not a shred of clothing on her."

"How is Inez?"

"She is in the hospital. They say she is hysterical."

"Poor girl," said one of the listeners. "She is doomed. Who will marry her now? It would be better if she died."

"We have to put a stop to these things," said a woman. "Today it's Inez. Who knows who will be next?"

Inez's father, Carlos, and his wife Anita, lodged a complaint with Flemingo, the village Regedor.

"What can I do?" he said.

"But Regedor-Bab," said Anita, with tears in her eyes, "you do understand our plight, don't you? You too have a daughter like mine. Today it's my daughter, tomorrow it might be yours."

Anger flashed on Flemingo's face. Placida was his only daughter, besought from Our Lady of Miracles, the patroness of the town of Mapuça. She had recently been betrothed to a young man from Orlim who was studying medicine in Portugal. She was often on her balcony, embroidering love slogans on pillow cases for her fiancé. Both father and mother doted on her and chaperoned her, lest anyone take advantage of her.

"How dare you say such a thing?" Flemingo roared.

"You can't imagine your daughter being raped, can you?" shrieked Anita. "Mine was and that doesn't concern you? My daughter won't get her virginity back, but I want justice for her. It's your job to give that."

Regedor Flemingo was furious at this fisherwoman's effrontery. At other times, he would have kicked her out of his house, but there was too much sympathy for her. In the end, he said lamely, "You can't blame the troops."

"They rape my daughter and you can't blame them! What kind of justice is this?" snapped Carlos.

Anita cried, "When Placida-Bae is raped not by whites but by black troops, then your eyes will be opened."

Images came into his mind of his daughter being raped by black troops. He slapped Anita, but when he calmed down, he realised that if his daughter were to be raped by Portuguese troops, he wouldn't be able to do anything either, and that frightened him. Something should be done. But what could he do? He couldn't lodge a complaint against the white troops, even though there was evidence.

"You know," he said, "I'm sorry about your girl and you are right that such a thing could happen to my daughter."

Carlos and Anita kept quiet.

"But why blame the troops? Were the troops in Goa before? No, we lived in peace. These troops wouldn't have been here if it weren't for some Goans who want the end of Portuguese rule. Stupid isn't it?"

"But why my daughter?" said Anita. "Inez never wanted to drive out the Portuguese."

"I know," said Flemingo. "It's only that... they don't have their women here... and after all, they are pacles, you know?"

"They have the right to rape our women? Is that what you're saying?" asked Carlos.

"It was wrong; I know that. But we must bear such things for our own good."

"Of course we should!" retorted Carlos. "When your daughter and your wife are raped then we'll see, Bab, how you bear it!"

Once again, images of white and black troops raping his wife and daughter blazed in Flemingo's mind, but though he hated himself as a spineless *canarim*, he ordered Carlos and Anita from his presence.

They approached senhor Furtado. He fully sympathised with them, but said he could do nothing to help them, because he didn't have any power. It was then that they approached Mario. They had heard him at Jozin-Bab's place and felt that at least he would understand their desire for justice.

"I'll do what I can," Mario promised when he had listened to their story. But after they had gone, he wondered how he could help. At the very least, he thought, the truth shouldn't be hidden; and he decided that the best way was to write an article on Inez's rape and submit it to the Goan papers.

Only *Vida*, the Goan Portuguese daily, accepted it. When it was published, it created a sensation. The article was carefully directed towards the civic values of the educated class and its tone was such that the Government couldn't write it off as inflammatory. Mario argued that the duty of good government was to maintain law and order and when law and order weren't kept, the duty of a good citizen was to make the Government aware of this fact. A good government must be pleased that a law-abiding citizen had made such facts known. It was from this point of view that he was writing. Inez's rape, and other rapes and molestations by the troops bred hatred towards the Government. If the Government wanted the goodwill of the people, it should investigate such allegations, punish those found guilty and put an end to such ugly occurrences.

The Government was caught in a fix. The tone of the article was so reasonable that they couldn't dismiss it as the work of an agitator, nor could they ignore it. An inquiry into the activities of the troops had to be conducted and the culprits would have to be brought to some semblance of a trial. That ought to be enough to save the Government's reputation. However, the Government was equally worried that the inquiry would boost Mario's prestige in the eyes of the Goan people. The Government believed that the nationalism transplanted from India would never have deep roots in Goa, but that a nationalism which grew from Goan issues would be altogether harder to uproot. So Mario Jaques went on their list of people to be watched.

An inquiry was held into Inez's rape; and she, now recovered, was asked to identify the culprits. Five white soldiers who had been in the truck that day were put before her. Though in the past she had always said that whites all looked the same to her, now she clearly attested that they were the same persons who had raped her

Some said that the inquiry was a farce, though others claimed that the culprits were court-martialled and sent to prison. But at least the Colonial Government curbed the undisciplined activities of the military and, for some time, people didn't hear of any further incidents of that nature. Anita and Carlos were grateful to Mario and people began to see him as a potential leader.

CHAPTER XX

But the Colonial Government also learned one half-effective lesson from the incident. They took *Vida* to task for publishing Mario's article and further clamped down on the press. Now, not a word could be published without clearing with the Government's censor. That didn't concern the mass of the people since only the elites read the papers, and their outlook was shaped by Government propaganda. But the people of Cavelossim and other villages nearby sang Mario's praises, and some of the older people remembered the stories told about his birth.

"Is it true," youngsters would ask Oji-mai Concentin, "that a shower of rain came on drought-stricken Goa exactly at the time of Mario's birth?"

"Yes, it did," she said. "Why should I tell you a lie? These very hands brought him into this world."

"And is it true that year had bountiful yields?"

"I can tell you this," she said, "the year Mario-Bab was born, no poor man went hungry; all had plenty to eat. Whatever Mario-Bab's faults may be, I know in my bones that he will deliver us from misery and want; deliver us from all evil. Wasn't it due to his efforts that the rapists of Inez were brought to book? What did Regedor-Bab do? Nothing. You call that one a Regedor? If a daughter of one of the batcars was raped, they would have surely done something. But Mario-Bab isn't like that. To him all are human, rich and poor alike."

All this praise for Mario was looked upon as a threat by the notables. Regedor Flemingo, for one, felt that his authority was being eroded. The Colonial Government didn't approve of Mario's popularity either, so they asked Flemingo to keep him under close observation and he was very happy to do so.

But the Government needed to do something more positive to win back the hearts and minds of the people, or at least do something to distract them. What would be better proof of how much the people needed them than to patch up the ancient feud between Carmona and Cavelossim? The notables of both villages were brought together and the Government proposed its plan. Though Carmona feebly objected, they were won over with the promise that the Government would give them a grant to renovate their dilapidated church and support some development schemes which the notables reckoned would put money in their pockets.

Senhor Tolentinho Furtado was the happiest man. The independence of Cavelossim, his life's dream, was handed to him on a silver platter. When the villagers came to know about it, they were happy, too. At long last they wouldn't be under the dominance of Carmona, and the Holy Cross, their tiny chapel, would be elevated to a church, the centre of a separate parish. The chaplain of Cavelossim was also a very happy man; he was sure that he would be elevated to being a vicar of the Holy Cross church.

The elites of Carmona persuaded the villagers to forget about the feud. Indeed, as the day of independence approached, they embraced one another as brothers. What had they all been fighting about? As the Government intended, the people's sense of grievance diminished, senhor Tolentinho was the hero of the hour, and Mario was no longer the focus of their hopes.

The date for the independence of Cavelossim was fixed for the 15th of August, 1947, the day Cavelossim always celebrated the Feast of Our Lady of Assumption. As the architect of Cavelossim's independence, senhor Tolentinho was given the honour of being the *prigent* of the celebrations. He had made history; he wanted to be remembered by posterity, and so he proposed that a marble monument should be build for him when he was gone. He even wrote his own epitaph in Portuguese, which in English went like this:

HERE LIES THE REMAINS OF
SENHOR THEDORIO TOLENTINHO FURTADO
BORN IN CAVELOSSIM IN THE YEAR OF OUR LORD, 1880 ON
THE 22ND OF JANUARY AND DIED IN THE YEAR OF OUR LORD.....
THE ONLY SON OF SENHOR JOÃO JOSÉ DO NACIMENTO FURTADO
AND OF SENHORA MARIA DE CEU BARBOSA E FURTADO
IT WAS DUE TO HIS TIRELESS EFFORTS THAT CAVELOSSIM
EMERGED AS AN INDEPENDENT VILLAGE AND PARISH ON THE
15TH DAY OF AUGUST, 1947.

The Carmona Communidade approved this plan and agreed to set a sum aside for its realisation. Senhor Tolentinho was even happier when he read articles in both Portuguese and Konkani dailies praising him as a sagacious leader who was instrumental in making Cavelossim a separate village. The newspapers also praised other elites both from Carmona and Cavelossim for their wisdom and maturity, and the gaocares from Carmona Communidade were so happy that they donated more money, five hundred rupees from its treasury, to celebrate the independence. The newspapers praised them even more for this gesture. Senhor Tolentinho wanted the 15th of August 1947 to be the most memorable day in the history of Cavelossim; and so, he persuaded the Confrarias of the Chaddos and the Sudras and the Fábrica to contribute money for the celebration of the occasion, which they willingly did.

The villagers of Cavelossim started celebrating their independence the day before the official date. Firecrackers exploded endlessly, people sang and danced outdoors and, in the pavilion, the village band played. At the stroke of midnight, the bell of the Holy Cross Church pealed on and on, proclaiming that it was no longer a chapel but a church. The villagers' hearts swelled with pride, tears in many eyes. Grenades boomed. Then the whole sky was lit with fireworks, more splendid than they had ever seen before.

As the sun came up on the day of independence, the whole village, dressed in their best, lined up on both sides of the red dirt road for the bishop to arrive. The bishop, a Portuguese, was the guest of honour. He was to celebrate the first mass in the Holy Cross Church. No one wanted to miss this opportunity; not only would the bishop bless the new church, but the people as well. Because the bishop was white and the Patriarch of God, his blessing had something extra special in it. What jubilation! What triumph when they saw his limousine approaching! The people were in sheer ecstasy; they felt as if Christ had stepped into their village. When the bishop got out of the limousine, the whole flock went down on their knees. Firecrackers exploded, grenades boomed, rockets illuminated the sky, and the village band played. The bishop was portly, about sixty years old. He had a white goatee and a moustache. He wore gold-rimmed spectacles and a red biretta. His raiment was red, and on his white body it looked radiant. He lifted his right hand and blessed the people, their heads bowed in humility. To some, the bishop offered his ring to kiss. Those lucky enough to do so were ecstatic, as if they had kissed the very hand of God. At long last, the former chaplain, now vicar, and other village dignitaries led the bishop into the church in grand procession.

It was ten in the morning. The Holy Cross Church was packed to capacity. Once again, the church bell rang and firecrackers exploded, announcing the beginning of solemn High Mass. In the church loft, the village choir sang divinely under the direction of the village maestro, Vicenti Mestri. Below, in the pews, Neunita Figueiredo, Mario's godmother, enunciated the rosary in Portuguese while the educated village girls joined in piously.

The bishop came to the pulpit. His homily was in Portuguese. He made reference to senhor Tolentinho and praised the elites of both Carmona and Cavelossim. And then he put this parable before them:

"Portugal is like a mustard seed." He looked at the elite among the audience and continued, "The Portuguese took the mustard seed and sowed it in Asia, Africa, America and throughout the world. Though it was the smallest seed, look at it now. It has grown, it is now the biggest tree, and today the birds of the air come to it for shelter. Goa is one of its branches – the most important branch in the East – the true Eastern capital of the Portuguese nation. Goans are among those birds that take shelter under Portugal – you are Portuguese!" He looked at the elites and the church dignitaries; their faces were lit up. They had understood him. Then, he looked at the commoners; they had perplexed looks on their faces. He put forth another parable.

"Again," said the bishop, and this time his voice was loud, "Portugal is like a fisherman casting a dragnet into the sea and hauling in all kinds of fish. When the net is full, the fishermen bring it ashore. Then they collect the good fish in the basket and throw the bad ones for the birds of the air or for the stray dogs to eat. Portugal will do likewise. Portugal will separate the good from the wicked. The wicked will be thrown into prisons, and they will weep and grind their teeth."

"What did Bishop *Saib* say in the sermon?" the serf woman Lucian asked Fernando Furtado, as they walked home from church.

"Lucian, the Bishop Saib said that all Goans are Portuguese and that Goa is the capital of the Portuguese nation in the East."

This didn't make any sense to Lucian. Fernando did his best to explain it to her. He felt it was his duty as a good Portuguese.

"It is a big honour for a Goan to be Portuguese," he said to her.

"A big honour to a serf woman like me?"

"Of course!"

"Does it mean I'll have a full belly?"

"You think only of your belly, don't you, Lucian?"

"Yes, Bab."

"Why, Lucian?"

"Mine is always empty. Yours is always full, Bab. So what else can I think of?"

"But man doesn't live by bread alone."

"But I do, Fernando Bab."

"Anyway," Fernando advised, "be a good Portuguese, otherwise you'll be thrown into prison. That's what Bishop Saib said."

"I'll try."

"Aren't you going to the dance, Lucian?" Fernando teased.

"No dances for me, Bab. But I'm going to Tolentinho Bab's house; he asked me help him."

Senhor Tolentinho was giving a banquet. To this only the most exalted were invited. The elites of Carmona and Cavelossim were there with their wives, the men dressed in swallow-tailed coats and striped trousers. The most exalted invitees were the Bishop and the other ecclesiastical authorities. Other colonial dignitaries – judges, advocates, administrators, captains, and civil servants – were also present, though the Governor-General, who was scheduled to attend, became indisposed at the last minute. Tolentinho's mansion had been given a facelift. It was whitewashed; the whole area around it was cleared of grass and bushes; the dirt path up to his house was paved so that the cars of the exalted could travel smoothly; the accumulated dust of ages had been got rid off; the rooms and salons were painted; the furniture was polished; the portraits of the ancestors were dusted; the giant Chinese vases that stood at the corners were cleaned, as were the chandeliers. Everything sparkled. Senhor Tolentinho glowed like a happy bridegroom. His two sisters, also dressed for the occasion, were nervous and shy but shared their brother's happiness. In the kitchen, Majancit and her aides laboured to make a grand banquet. It evidently made a very good impression on the bishop, who ate a great deal of food and drank a good quantity of wine. He would now and then come to the balcony and raise his hand and bless the crowd gathered outside. The multitude would go on their knees and bow their heads. This prince of the church had made them very happy.

But senhor Tolentinho's banquet wasn't the only function in the village. The youths from the wealthier families had organised a soirée – *Festa de Flores*. Under the guidance of Flinto Soares, the expert, they had put up a big tent in an uncultivated field and had decorated it beautifully. The floor was watered and pounded to make it smooth, then strewn with tiny green leaves to allow the dancing couples to glide gracefully. From the white cloth-ceiling hung lanterns; it wasn't quite electricity, but the powerful new petromax lamps rented from goldsmith Gopinath almost allowed you to think so.

In the corner was Migel's band – *Banda Ultramar* – the best in Salcete. The tent was packed and the couples danced to the soft music, mostly waltzes. Because this was a special soirée, senhor Tolentinho was asked to raise the toast, and though he was exhausted, he came. Banda Ultramar played a special tune to welcome him – *La em cima está Tio Salazar*. Standing among the revellers, tall and erect with a champagne glass in his hand, Tolentinho raised a toast for independent Cavelossim.

"Ladies and gentlemen," he said in Portuguese, his voice resonant, "Today isn't only the day of our Feast, but also the day of our Independence. Today, is a day of our happiness. We are very, very happy today because Cavelossim, our tiny village, is free! Free!... Viva! Viva! Viva!"

Senhor Tolentinho gulped his champagne for the happiness of independent Cavelossim; the others followed suit. The whole tent resounded with vivas, and outside firecrackers exploded nonstop. Senhor Tolentinho didn't stay long, but the revellers danced until the sun came up.

There were other entertainments. A soccer match was held between Carmona and Cavelossim; it was a friendly contest, no one minded who won. There was also a bull fight, but again it was a friendly contest. Yet a grand occasion like this couldn't finish without a *theatr*. Domaceano Da Costa, the village theatrist, had organised the village talent and was ready to put on the premiere of his new play, *The Birth of a New Village*. With his fertile imagination, he depicted the struggle of Cavelossim's people to make their village independent from Carmona. It recognised the role of senhor Tolentinho in the struggle and many songs eulogized him, the Bishop and the Colonial Government. In the last scene, the main character delivered a monologue:

"The independence of Cavelossim is a miracle! Why? Because the Holy Cross, the patron saint of our village, heard our prayers. It's the Cross who put in the minds of the ecclesiastical authorities the idea of elevating our chapel to a church. Hence, my fellow villagers, we should never be ungrateful to the Holy Cross. Have faith in the Holy Cross and He will never abandon you. Pray to Him and He will answer your prayers. Never, never forget that. I ask all villagers of Cavelossim to wear a crucifix around their necks. That indeed will please the Holy Cross. Won't you do that?"

"We will," the audience shouted back.

Before the curtain fell, he said, "If you haven't a crucifix, buy one; and even if you have one, buy one today for they are sanctified by His Holiness, the Bishop of Goa. They are on sale at the door as you go out."

The audience applauded until their hands were red. The theatr was over, as were the celebrations, and the people of Cavelossim, who'd had one of the best days in their lives, went to their beds to get a good rest.

But no one had seen Mario all day.

CHAPTER XXI

When the villagers awoke the next morning, the first thing they
heard was that Mario had been arrested. Yesterday's festivities soon
ceased to be the main topic of conversation.

"But why?" someone asked Alvito Santos, a student in the
English secondary school who had seen Mario's arrest.

"I don't know."

"But you saw it, didn't you?"

"I did," Alvito Santos began, "I was at Bombi's restaurant. Mario
was there too, and we were listening to Nehru's independence speech
on Bombi's battery-operated radio."

"Yes," another said. "What a coincidence! India too became free
on the 15th of August, just like Cavelossim."

"As I was saying," Alvito Santos continued, "we were listening to
Nehru saying, 'At the stroke of the midnight hour, when the world
sleeps, India will awake to life and freedom.' And I heard Mario say,
'The days of colonialism all over the world are numbered.' Hardly,
had he said that, when, as if from nowhere, a military jeep arrived and
stopped at Bombi's restaurant. Something is wrong, I said to myself.
I was frightened. Bombi turned the radio off. Then three white
soldiers stepped out of the jeep and among them was one Goan. They
all came into the restaurant."

"One Goan? You know him?"

"Madeu, the son of a businessman from Margão. He's the one who
identified Mario."

"Couldn't Mario escape?"

"There wasn't time and even if there was, I don't think Mario
would have. They asked, 'Are you Mario Jaques?' and he said, 'Yes.'
Then they handcuffed him, put him in their jeep and drove off."

When Rosa Jaques heard the news she swooned and fell.
Unconscious, she saw her terrible vision of Mario on the cross. She
saw blood dripping from his hands and from his other wounds. It
seemed to her that the cross held him in an embrace and she shouted
at it, "You get away from my son! Release him this instant! You,
constipated bitch; do you hear me?"

She was crying out as she came to in Maximiano's arms. He said, suppressing his own tears, "Rosa, our son will be safe, he'll be released."

That afternoon, Maximiano and Rosa went to Margão's police station. After bribing a policeman, they discovered that Mario was detained there; bribing another policeman, they got an appointment to see *Chefe* Vasquito, who was in charge of Mario's case. He was a light-skinned, short, fat mestiço, but Goan to the core; he drank feni, wolfed down Goan food and spat Goan obscenities when angry. Recently, he had been promoted to the task of suppressing the nationalist movement. He had done a good job filling the prisons.

When at last Rosa and Maximiano were ushered into his office, they felt like frightened children. Getting up from his chair, with all courtesy, Vasquito spoke to Rosa in Portuguese:

"Please sit down, lady. You have come to see Mario?"

"Yes."

His eyes full of pity, he said, "I have children too. But, sometimes children are crosses, aren't they?"

Rosa and Maximiano did not respond.

"Sometimes, it's better not to have children at all. Mario will take you both to your graves before your time."

Hesitantly, Rosa asked, "Why do you say that, Chefe?"

"Well," he said, "I was proud of your son when I read his article in *Vida*. I didn't like what the troops were doing to our women folk. But Mario committed the same sin."

"What sin?" Maximiano asked.

"Don't you know? He made a girl called Nirmala Karapurkar pregnant."

"Did what?" Maximiano shouted.

Silence fell. Maximiano was stunned, as if by a heavy hammer blow to his head. Rosa froze. The Chefe's eyes were on them; he knew what was going on in their minds. Their son had soiled the moral code of the society, Hindu or Catholic. He had dumped their name into a cesspool and they were like worms wriggling in that dung. Who would marry that girl now? Mario had to. But Nirmala was a Hindu and Mario a Catholic...

"And the worst thing is..." said Vasquito. "He says, he never made her pregnant."

"What does Nirmala say?"

He shifted his gaze from Rosa to Maximiano; they felt that he was going to throw another bombshell at them.

"Nirmala wasn't bold enough to face her disgrace," he said. "She soaked herself in gasoline and when there was no one around to stop her, she set fire to herself in the compound."

This was too much for Maximiano. Everything before him was receding; he fell from the chair and everything went dark.

"Call a doctor," Rosa cried. "Doctor please! Doctor!"

Chefe Vasquito at once dispatched his subordinate to call a doctor. When the doctor arrived, he examined Maximiano while Rosa took out her rosary and prayed to Our Lady of Perpetual Succour, asking her not to take her husband away. When the doctor had finished diagnosing Maximiano, Rosa was still clutching her rosary.

"Is he....?" she asked, fearfully.

"He's in a critical condition."

"But he's going to live?"

"I'm not God."

"What's the prognosis, doctor?" Vasquito asked.

"He's suffered a stroke."

Maximiano was put onto a stretcher and carried to the Hospital do Hospicio in Margão. Despite Rosa's strong faith in Our Lady of Perpetual Succour, she also pleaded with the miraculous Christ of Varcá to restore her husband's health, promising him four candles. After a long wait, a nurse came and told her that she could see her husband. She went to his room, held his hand and poured out her soul to him, even though he was still unconscious. When a nurse came and told her that she should leave, she insisted that she should stay, but the nurse said, "He's in good hands. You go home now, take some rest and come tomorrow."

Before she left, she looked at her husband and kissed him on the cheek. It was dark when she came out. Where was her home? Her only son was in prison and her husband in hospital. She walked to the bus stand, fingering her rosary beads. She caught the last bus to Cavelossim. Some of the villagers were still about when she arrived.

"Did you see Mario, Rosa?" Eloise, one of the village women asked. She took Rosa's hand and said, "Whoever would have thought Mario would turn out like this? You must know that they found Nirmala's mother drowned in a well. And just now, I heard in the bus that the old man, Vitol Karapurkar, Nirmala's grandfather, died of a heart attack."

Rosa had pledged that nothing else should touch her. Her whole concern was for her husband, and not Mario. She heard whispers that

Mario was a murderer — the man who brought a holocaust on Vitol's household. It was true; he was taking her husband, his own father to the grave. Yes, he was a murderer. But what could she do about that?

"Mario is dead and buried!" she said to Eloise. "But I am worried about my husband."

"Where is Maximiano-Bab?" Modo-mai Majakin asked.

With tears and sobs Rosa narrated all that had happened. Modo-mai was distraught. Maximiano was like her son; she had given him her breasts to suck when he was a baby. They lit the candles before the oratorio and prayed for his recovery.

Though she made no plans to visit Mario, Rosa learnt that he was incarcerated in Aguada prison. It was the Cross, that harlot, who had seduced Mario to tread the path to Golgotha, and she had no power over the Cross. Her only concern was her husband, he was the only one she had now, and she went everyday to visit him. Despite her rosaries and vows to the saints, her husband hadn't yet regained consciousness. But one morning, as she was by his side, she heard him say, "Rosa!"

She was so happy that she could hardly talk. Maximiano had come out of the coma, and was looking tenderly at her. She took his hand, but still no words came. Her eyes brimmed when she heard him say, "How's our son?"

She told him that she hadn't gone to see Mario; she didn't want to tell him anything else. "Forget about Mario, I want to talk about you. How do you feel?"

Maximiano's eyes shone with love and her own heart thumped with love. She gave a sigh of relief; the scare was over, her husband was going to be well.

Before the bell rang telling visitors it was time to leave, Maximiano asked Rosa to visit Mario in prison. She didn't want to, but to please her husband she said she would.

Next day, when Rosa came to the hospital, she saw her husband's bed empty. Her heart stopped beating for a few seconds, but pushing her panic aside, she asked the nurse, "Where's my husband?"

"I'm very sorry," the nurse said gently, "he passed away in his sleep last night."

Mario couldn't understand why Nirmala had committed suicide. Lying on a wooden plank, he would torment himself thinking about it. Sometimes, it was even a relief when, late in the night, he was taken from his cell and beaten with a rubber truncheon. His tormentor, seeing the glint in Mario's eyes, as if he were gaining satisfaction from it, would get puzzled.

One morning, Chefe Vasquito came to see him. "We're going for a drive, Mario," he said.

Mario was handcuffed and brought out. The daylight hurt his eyes. A police car was waiting. Where were they taking him?

"Get into the car!" Vasquito ordered him. "You murderer!"

Vasquito drove the car. Mario sat in the back, flanked by two policemen. They passed Panjim and came to Cortalim. Here, the car took the ferry across the river Zuari; the passengers looked at Mario and talked in whispers. After the crossing, they drove to Margão and from there the car sped on the maroon road to Cavelossim. As they drove, Mario saw some familiar faces going with their wares to Margão: fisher-women with baskets on their heads, their buttocks swaying as they hurried to the market; carpenters with their tools; and then, he saw Cursin, the jack-of-all-trades, his neighbour. With his familiar trot, head down, hurrying, his pockets seemed to be stuffed with sheaves of envelopes. Letters. Something was wrong. Death? Was it his mother, his father? Mario called out to Cursin, but the car sped on. Finally, when the car stopped before his house, he saw a crowd of people. When they saw him they fell silent. The policemen shoved him from the car and there he stood – handcuffed, unshaven, long, dishevelled hair, almost a skeleton. As he stood there, he heard his mother call out in grief.

Chefe Vasquito approached him and said, "See what you've done! You killed your own father, too!"

The people looked at Mario silently. When Neunita Figueiredo came from the house, she passed him without saying a word, as if he didn't exist at all. But Hut João, his godfather, came and embraced him. Mario, who was handcuffed, couldn't embrace him in return. Placing his head on Hut João's shoulder, he wept like a small child, and Hut João, his eyes streaming, consoled him, patting him on the back. As Hut João was retreating, Mario's eyes fell on Oji-mai Concentin. She stood and looked at him; she was confused. She didn't know what Mario was. Once she thought she had delivered a cherub; but now the civil and church authorities proclaimed him the incarnation of a devil. She walked away. But as if from nowhere, Modo-mai Majakin came and she pressed him tight to her drooping bosom; she had been a wet-nurse to his father, and it was as if Mario was her grandson. Releasing him from her embrace, she said, "Come my morgado," and they entered the house.

In the family prayer room, Mario saw his father laid out in a black coffin, dressed in a black suit. On benches, on both sides of the coffin, · sat the women. Among them was Rosa. Her hair was spread on her shoulders, her eyes were red and swollen, her hands bare of bangles and her ear-lobes without ear-rings. She looked at Mario, her bosom heaving, and Mario looked at her, all choked up. They didn't utter a word or a cry, but Rosa opened her arms and beckoned to him. He came and she embraced him so tightly, as if she had lost him and then found him again. He wanted to say that he was the cause of all this pain, but words wouldn't come. Releasing him, she looked at him and then shifted her gaze to her husband. She beckoned Mario to sit by her side and he did. Looking at his father in the coffin, he saw a touch of a smile on his father's face, as if he had been happy to die.

Hours went by and the moment came when the coffin was about to be closed. Rosa embraced Mario. He cried out, "Mother!"

The cry triggered her grief to boom out like monsoon thunder and her tears fell like monsoon rain, while Mario remained in her embrace, sobbing, not knowing how to console her.

The priest raised his voice in Latin chant, starting the funeral service, and Rosa's wailing stopped. Mario became calmer as he heard the priest chanting, *"Requiem aeternam dona dei, Domine: et lux pertetua ei."*

These words touched him, and for a time he was lost in thought. When his attention returned, he cried, "Oh Lord, grant unto my father eternal rest and let Thy perpetual light shine upon him."

The village priest and the funeral guests looked at him. Rosa, Majakin, Concentin, Hut João and others whispered 'Amen'.

The lid was put on the coffin and the pallbearers took their places. Because Mario was one of the pallbearers, his handcuffs were unlocked, but the policeman stood by his side lest he run away. Along with others, Mario carried his father, and as the funeral procession marched, he could hear *Our Father* being chanted, and its cadences fell like ever growing drops of rain into his mind until the deluge washed away his consciousness and he fell to the ground. Someone took his place and the funeral procession marched on.

When Mario came to, he heard the priest chanting in Latin; looking around, he knew he was in the church. He had once been an altar boy, and it was in this same church he had done his best to communicate with God, but God had never answered. It was then he had drunk the mass-wine and swallowed the consecrated wafers, and gone home shouting that there was no God. As he was recalling this incident, his father's coffin was brought to the centre of the church and set on a podium, the feet facing the altar. The lid of the coffin was taken off and Mario looked yearningly at his father. The priest came down from the altar and walked round the coffin twice. The first time, he sprinkled it with holy water, the second time he wafted it with incense. The priest sang:

> *Et ne nos inducas in tentationem*
> *Sed libera nos a malo*
> *A porta inferi.*
> *Erue, Domine, animan ejus*
> *Requiescat in pace*
> *Amen.*

As the priest was singing the Latin chant, Mario's vision of paradise returned. Before the body of his father, he pledged that he would deliver the people from evil and close the gates of hell forever.

As the ritual in the church came to an end, Antonio, the sacristan, closed the coffin. Now the procession marched to the cemetery.

His father's grave was on the right-hand side, near the cistern. Even in the cemetery there were classes; here the brahmin, the chaddo, the sudra and the outcast came to their separate final resting places, turned into the same coloured dust. Mario thought that men were like worms fighting to eat a corpse and then fighting to eat each other. They had to build a society based not on exploitation but on love. As such thoughts went through his mind, he heard the priest say: "*Ego sum resurrection et vita: et omnis qui vivit et credit in Me, non morietur in aeternum.*"

The coffin was opened once more and Mario felt drawn to his father like an iron nail to a magnet. Before the coffin was sealed for good, Mario kissed his father on his forehead. The priest's voice rose as he sprinkled the coffin with the holy water: "*Et ne nos inducas in tetationem.*"

As the coffin was being lowered into the grave, Mario cried, "Father! Father! Father!"

"*Oremus*," said the priest. "Grant to Thy servant Maximiano..."

"Father..." Mario was sobbing like a child. Hut João, his godfather, put his arms around him, comforting him.

"*Requiescat in pace*," said the priest.

"Amen," said Mario along with others.

Mario heard the clod of earth thud on the coffin and the thud echoed within him. At that moment he felt drawn to his father as never before. He was his father's flesh. He took earth in his hands and put it on his father's coffin, the others following him. They were reminded again that man is nothing but dust and to dust he returns.

After the service, Mario stood by the gate of the cemetery and the mourners paid him condolences, then they left to go to his house. Rosa, hearing them come, cried a dirge and when it had subsided, the village elder, Caetano D'Costa, announced the prayers to the departed soul of Maximiano. When it was over, Cursin and Tar Menin served two goblets of feni to the funeral participants.

Mario had to leave. Handcuffed again, he looked at his mother. He looked at all the people there. He loved them. He had thought once that they were the beads of a rosary bound by love. The light of the kerosene lamps in the house looked dismal and everything around him was sad. Before leaving he said, "Mother, I love you."

"You are the only one I've got now, Mario," she said.

Chefe Vasquito blew the horn of the car.

Mario kissed his mother and looked at Modo-mai Majakin, Oji-mai Concentin, Ermelin and others who were with her.

"Don't worry Mario-Bab," said Modo-mai Majakin. "We'll look after your mother. You take care."

Mario was pushed into the car and driven to his cell at Aguada.

CHAPTER XXII

Though Mario knew that most people looked upon him as the worst kind of criminal, he could not feel responsible for all the deaths he had been blamed for. Could he have set in motion the chain of reactions? This was surely God's doing, but a god with divergent personalities, each clashing with the other. In this case the Saraswat brahmin personality of God clashed with the Catholic personality of God, killing Nirmala, her mother, her grandfather and his father. God who boasts that he created man in his image had wantonly killed these people. What kind of a god was this? Nirmala and he had wanted to give up this god, but this grotesque god had taken her away from him. But as he thought of Nirmala, he remembered holding her in his arms on the Monte. He sensed her presence, her touch, not physical, but her presence none the less. A calm embraced him and he slept soundly.

"Wake up," he heard the next morning.

Mario saw that the prison guard wasn't the usual one. He was a firngo like the former, but seemed friendly.

"What's your name?" Mario asked.

"Abel Pinto."

As days went by, a friendship developed between them. Abel's duty started at ten at night and ended at six in the morning. Often in the night, Abel would come with offerings of cheese, cream-crackers, a can of sardines, fruit and other foods from the military canteen and they would eat and talk. Sometimes, they would hear screams and they knew that a prisoner was being tortured.

"Horrible," Abel would say.

"Didn't you ever torture a prisoner?" Mario asked.

"You must understand," Abel said, "I never wanted to be in the army. But it's compulsory for all males. I couldn't escape. But my brother did. He ran away to France."

"Why couldn't you?"

"My mother was ill and there was nobody to look after her. And besides, I was being watched."

"How is your mother now?"

"Only yesterday I got a letter from her. She's in good health. You asked me if I'd tortured prisoners; to be honest, I have, and sometimes I still have to, even though it's against my conscience. If I don't, I know what's in store for me. At the beginning I was indoctrinated. I was happy to do the will of Dr. Salazar."

"What changed you?"

"Political systems enslave our minds. If we are comfortable and secure within a system, we defend the system by any means. We fear that if the system is destroyed, we are destroyed. Isn't that so?"

"I think, it is."

"The Portuguese ruling class try to convince us that they are our benefactors, but in reality they wean us away from our inborn morality and capacity for love. They make us hate those who oppose us, who don't belong to our pack."

"We have to resist such lures," said Mario. "Man has to go back to his true nature. Man is truly human when he is bound to other humans by love, not by politics or religion."

"That's easier said than done," said Abel. "We're products of our age."

"I understand that," said Mario. "The man within the political system will do everything to destroy the man who steps outside it. Do you think that I'll be strong enough?"

"Strong enough for what?"

"Strong enough to work for the betterment of mankind. Or will I despair if no one takes me seriously. Will I give up my vision if I'm rejected and unloved?"

"I don't know, man, I don't know myself. Though I'm troubled by my situation, I have no will to change anything. I go with the herd. And yet there has been some change in me – you asked me just now how that change came about."

"I did."

"I'm in love." Abel told Mario that he loved a woman called Serafina Barbosa who came from an aristocratic brahmin Catholic family of Benaulim, so proud that even though he was a firngo, the Barbosas looked down on him, especially Serafina's cleric-brother. "Serafina's elders are like Portuguese *fidalgos* and they have table manners like them. Serafina's father is an *advagado*, her uncle is a monsignor and the other is a *cirugião* in Portugal; and yet, they are Goans rather than Portuguese. They don't want Serafina to marry me because I'm a Portuguese. It's their Goanness that stands in my way to marry Serafina, whatever Salazar says about Goans being Portuguese."

"I think you're right," Mario said. "How did you meet Serafina?"

"She was my teacher."

"Your teacher!"

"Yes. Many of us Portuguese don't know how to read and write. You educated Goans talk and write better Portuguese than we do, and many of you talk and write English as well. But you asked what changed me. It's Serafina's love that changed me. She not only prepared me for the *Segundo Grau* examination, she introduced me to many writers and all those soaked into my soul. I read Tagore in Portuguese. I began to look at mankind in a different way. I saw how political parties, nations, groups and other organisations operate. They are all bullies who divide mankind. But in the true spirit of love, Mario, there aren't walls. Serafina's love made me understand that. Make space for love to grow, only then we'll be one."

It was already morning. They heard a village rooster crowing, and the fishermen calling as they hauled in the nets down below the Aguada Fort.

"I'm sorry to keep you so late," said Abel.

"That's O.K." Mario said. "You're a godsend. Without you, I don't know how I would survive."

"We'll talk again," said Abel. "But I'd better let you get some sleep."

Because of his reputation as an agitator, Mario was confined to a solitary cell. Rosa didn't know this and she was shocked to find that she wasn't allowed to see him.

"Why?" she asked the guard.

"Those are the orders."

"Whose orders?"

"Orders from the authorities."

Though trained in submission to church, state and husband, Rosa wasn't going to take this kind of nonsense. No one could stop her from seeing her son. Next day, she went to see *Capitão* Braz Pinto, Chief of the Goan Police in Panjim. Here, too, she was turned away. By chance, though, at that moment Capitão Pinto arrived in his car and seeing her protesting loudly at the gate, he asked the guard what the disturbance was about.

"She wants to see you, Capitão."

"See me?".

Rosa looked at him. Though he was dressed in his khaki uniform, he seemed to her to have a kind face.

"Come in," he said, smiling, leading her to his sitting room. "Sit down please," he said. "I'll be with you soon."

"Good morning!" said Mrs. Braz Pinto coming into the sitting room. "Can my husband help you in any way?"

"I hope so." Rosa answered.

"Let me get you a cup of coffee," Mrs. Pinto insisted. "My husband is in the shower. He'll be with you soon. Have a cup of coffee and in the meantime you can share your woes with me."

Rosa was touched and, sipping her coffee, she opened her heart to Mrs. Pinto.

"You don't think that your son made the Hindu girl pregnant?" asked Mrs. Pinto.

"Certainly not," answered Rosa.

"Then, who made her pregnant?"

"I don't think anybody made her pregnant. There isn't any proof that she was pregnant."

"Then why did she commit suicide?"

"For that we must understand the Goan mind. But my son never made Nirmala pregnant."

At this moment, Capitão Pinto returned to the sitting room. Mrs. Pinto immediately told him Rosa's story. Rosa watched Pinto's eyes flickering as he listened.

"You really don't think so?"

"I don't think so, I know so," said Rosa, finishing her coffee. "Mario didn't make Nirmala pregnant."

"But he is a nationalist?" asked Pinto.

"I don't know what he is," said Rosa. " But certainly, he isn't a rapist. So why am I not allowed to visit my own son?"

"I'll do what I can," said Pinto, before dismissing her.

Capitão Pinto kept his word. Within two weeks, a police jeep came to her house. The villagers, looking from their windows, thought the worst.

"Why are you arresting her?" asked Modo-mai Majakin who had come running.

"Moda-mai," said Rosa, "they aren't arresting me. They're taking me to see Mario."

"Are you sure?"

"Yes, Modo-mai. Here is the key to the house. Please feed the pig. Don't worry about me. I'll bring you the news of your morgado."

Modo-mai watched as Rosa left, then went to light candles in the oratorio and prayed that Rosa would come to no harm. Who could trust the police these days?

Capitão Pinto, in the meantime, had removed Mario from solitary confinement and had put him in a bigger cell with other political prisoners. Here he met other Goan nationalists whom the colonial government had branded as bandits and terrorists.

"Do you know what this cell is called?" asked Roque Santan when they were introduced. He was recovering from bullet wounds received when he was distributing revolutionary pamphlets.

"No," answered Mario.

"Welcome to *Cela de Liberdade.*"

Ravi, another political prisoner, introduced him to Polly de Silva, who looked more like an intellectual than a revolutionary.

"What is he in for?" Mario asked Ravi afterwards.

"Polly sent a bomb in a book through registered post to Judge Quadros as a punishment for sentencing Goan nationalists to harsh imprisonments. It wasn't a big blast, but the judge lost some fingers."

"But how did they find out that it was sent by Polly?"

"Polly couldn't resist taking credit for his action. While he was in Chinchinim market – he comes from Chinchinim – he blabbed about it to his friends. The fool didn't know that even among his friends there were Portuguese spies. So he was arrested and the clerk at Margão Post Office, who registered the parcel, identified him."

In this way, Mario came to know every prisoner in the cell. Often, they would discuss politics and many of them thought that they would be in power once Goa was free from Portuguese rule. Many were frustrated because Nehru wouldn't march his troops on Goa, believing that Indian intervention would be the quickest route to freedom. Mario listened carefully to these debates, but never voiced his opinion and they never bothered to ask it. In their eyes he wasn't a freedom fighter but a sexual offender.

"Someone has a visitor," said Cardoso, another political prisoner.

Mario was astonished to see his mother being escorted into the cell. Rosa, tears streaming from her eyes, ran and hugged him. Eventually, releasing him from her embrace, she inspected him from head to toe. "How thin you are my son!"

"I'm fine, mother."

Mario introduced her to the other inmates. To Rosa they seemed like decent young men and not hardened criminals as Portuguese propaganda claimed. Though Rosa didn't know their offences, she sensed that they too had their visions, like her son.

"It's time," said the escort. Before leaving Rosa hugged Mario again.

"Mother," said one of the inmates. "When you come next time, be sure to bring us some sweetmeats."

"Sure," she said.

All the way home, Rosa thought about Mario and his comrades in prison. Though she didn't understand them, she knew they had dreams. The Cross, she thought, was a hussy flirting with so many young men. Why couldn't Mario see that?

Late in the evening Rosa arrived home. Modo-Mai was anxiously waiting for her. She eagerly asked Rosa about Mario and Rosa told her everything.

"I haven't seen you so happy for a long time," said Modo-mai.

"I am happy, Modo-mai," answered Rosa. "I think in the end everything will turn out all right."

CHAPTER XXIII

On the village roads, jeeps loaded with stern-faced soldiers zoomed by. Villagers were afraid to talk even in whispers. Dictator Salazar was everywhere in their consciousness. In reality, Salazar's power in Goa was in its death throes. In the agony of desperation, his soldiers fired on peaceful Goans and Indians when they offered satyagraha to free Goa from Colonial rule. This provoked many Goan youths to confront violence with violence, and these crossed the border and joined Azad Gomantak Dal in Belgaum under the leadership of Vishwanath Lawande. They would come to Goa under the cover of the night and blow up military posts and police stations. The colonial regime did all they could to prevent the villagers from joining the struggle, herding them into the soccer grounds every weekend, and counting them like a cattle. Everywhere around the stadiums, lifesize portraits of Salazar and Caveiro Lopes, the President of Portugal kept an eye on them. After the gathering had been silenced, the Regedor or sometimes a higher colonial officer would address them, his voice booming through the loudspeakers, praising the colonial authority for bestowing so many favours upon Goans, but also dishing out stern warnings. Salazar, Caveiro Lopes and Alvarnaz, the Patriarch of Goa and the Orient, were like a Trinity and, like God, they knew even the villagers' unformed thoughts. And, they were told, as long as the relic of Saint Francisco Xavier was in Goa, no one would dare invade *Estado da India*.

But when Dadara and Nagar-Avali, Portuguese enclaves inside India, fell to Goan nationalists based in Bombay, doubts arose in the people's minds. In the stadiums they were told that God had always aided Portugal, and He wouldn't desert her now. Lifting their hearts and souls they chanted *Te Deum* and *Herois do Mar*. As they sang, some Catholics claimed that they saw the archangel Michael at the head of an army of angels coming down to earth. Not to be outdone, some Hindus said that they had seen Lord Krishna descending to earth. The help of these celestial deities was only to be expected, Portuguese propaganda claimed, for wasn't Salazar no less a deity than they?

Nehru, in keeping with his nonviolent, pacifist image, sanctioned an economic blockade. Since the Goan economy had always depended for its imports and exports on the markets of the Indian Union and because many Goans depended on India for work, the blockade ought to have been effective, but closing the frontiers didn't bring the desired effects. God seemed indeed to favour Salazar. At this time, the Goan mining industry had its first boom and many ships called at Mormugão harbour to load iron ore. The colonial government could now play guardian angel. The salaries of civil servants and even labourers' wages rose higher than their expectations, and to meet this new demand, Goa was flooded with foreign goods, bringing prosperity to both Goan and Indian smugglers.

But the blockade brought misery to some, mostly those who worked in the Indian Union. They couldn't visit their dependants without a travel document and it wasn't easy to get these from the Indian bureaucracy. Goans who wanted to get into India and Goans from the Indian Union who wanted to get into Goa had to pay a lot of money to those who were ready to smuggle them across the border. Many fell victims to accidents, others were robbed and women who went to join their husbands were raped. Often, if they made it into the Indian Union, they were caught by the Indian police and thrown back into Goa. Goans who earned their living in the Indian Union couldn't send money back to their dependants. Underground agents sprang up on both sides, charging high commissions in both directions. Regedor Flemingo of Cavelossim and Baltazar Afonso of Carmona both acted as agents and prayed to their favourite saints that Portugal would always rule Goa and the nonviolent Nehru would never lift the blockade.

Early one morning, Regedor Flemingo came in a jeep with white soldiers and pounded furiously on Rosa's door.

"*Kon tinga cheddechea* – What bastard's there?" Modo-mai, who was keeping Rosa company, screeched.

"Open the door! Open the door!" Regedor bellowed.

When Rosa opened the door and saw Regedor Flemingo with white soldiers, her face went pallid with fear.

"Where are you hiding Mario?" Regedor Flemingo demanded, pushing Rosa aside. The white soldiers went from room to room looking everywhere, under beds, in the bathroom, toilet and granary.

"What are you looking for?" Modo-mai asked.

"Where are you hiding him?"

"Hiding whom?"

"Mario!"

"Isn't he in Fort Aguada?"

"He escaped!"

The village was now awake and alarmed to see Rosa and Modo-mai being taken away in the jeep. Later, at mass, the vicar told them that Mario had escaped from prison. "As I've always told you, Mario is nothing but evil. The Devil abides in him."

That evening, at the mass gathering at Cavelossim, Regedor Flemingo told the crowd that Mario had escaped but that he would certainly be caught. He was a very dangerous criminal and people who helped him would be in serious trouble. At the end of his oration, photographs of Mario were distributed, and posters describing him as a WANTED CRIMINAL were nailed up in the market places. All the dailies carried Mario's photo on their front pages and *Emissora de Goa* broadcast news of Mario's escape every fifteen minutes, warning the people that it was their duty to report him to any police station if they knew of his whereabouts. Secretly many admired his daring and the elites were mystified.

"No one has ever escaped from Fort Aguada," said the vicar, an authority on such matters. "I tell you, Mario is the Devil's agent and only with the Devil's powers could he have escaped from prison." Some of the notables believed this, since no other explanation made sense.

Rosa and Modo-mai were taken to the Margão police station and interrogated by Rudolfo Coelho, a Goan police officer. He cajoled them and threatened them, but when he was certain that they didn't know anything about Mario's escape, he let them go.

"But where's my son?" Rosa demanded.

"Shut up!" retorted Rudolfo Coelho, who was so angry that he began to scratch his balding head and fidget with his testicles.

"You pig!" Modo-mai shouted. "Didn't your mother teach you anything?"

"Where's my son?" Rosa screamed. "Have you killed him?"

"Get them out of here!" Coelho pleaded to his subordinate.

But how had Mario escaped? Why wasn't he found yet? The people weren't fools; they thought he'd been killed and that the colonial authorities were making all this noise to cover up their crime.

Rosa didn't know what to believe, but one evening, she broke down crying, " Mario! Mario! You were the gift of the Holy Cross. After how many vows and prayers and lit candles were you conceived! Listen, all of you who are now treating me like a leper, have you forgotten? Have you?"

"Calm down, Ocobae," Modo-mai pleaded.

But Rosa went on, "All of you would have starved to death! You ungrateful people! And now, he's killed! Who killed him? Men like Regedor Flemingo killed him! My son isn't a rapist! He was framed! He was framed!"

"Ocobae, please calm down," Modo-mai begged. "If the Regedor hears this, he'll come with his soldiers."

"Let him come! Let him come!" screamed Rosa. "I'll cut off his prick and send him home!"

Modo-mai was shocked to hear Rosa talk like this, but she understood her grief. Rosa went on shouting and moaning until she was spent and Modo-mai put her to bed. As sleep took her over, Rosa dreamt that Maximiano spoke to her.

"Why are you wasting yourself in grief, *meu amorsinho*? Our Mario isn't dead," he said, and then he was gone.

"Mario is alive! Mario is alive!" shouted Rosa coming out of her dream.

"I knew it," said Modo-mai. "They could not get rid of my morgado so easily."

Next day, Regedor Flemingo ordered all the villagers to attend a mass meeting in the evening. When all were there, Flemingo announced, "My fellow villagers, Mario has escaped to the Indian Union."

Hush fell upon the audience.

He continued, "I'm ashamed that he comes from Cavelossim! I'm ashamed that he's a Goan! He raped Nirmala, he killed her, he killed her mother, her grandfather and his own father! What a monster! Could there be a worse criminal than Mario?"

"Never!" someone shouted, giving the cue to the crowd, and they all shouted, "Never! Never! Never!"

As the shouting subsided, Regedor Flemingo resumed, "The vicar has told us that the Devil abides in Mario, and I have no doubt about it. It's with the Devil's help that Mario escaped. And I have something else to tell you." Here, tears trickled from his eyes and his voice choked, "It's been confirmed that his guard, Abel Pinto, a brave Portuguese soldier, was shot dead by Mario."

The audience fell into silence.

After a brief pause, Regedor Flemingo raged, "The Indian Union might shelter him, but God will get him; and if He doesn't, I'll get him and tear him into pieces."

Then he asked them to be silent for a minute in memory of Abel Pinto. Before they went home, *Herois do Mar*, the Portuguese national anthem, was sung.

CHAPTER XXIV

At much the same time as Regidor Flemingo was slandering his name, Mario was at the police compound in Castle Rock, in the Indian Union, giving a detailed account of his escape.

In the middle of the night, someone had caught his arm, dragging him from his bed. He couldn't make out who it was until he recognised Abel Pinto's voice. Abel had taken him to the guards' toilet and told him to put on a uniform he'd concealed there. Then he and Abel had walked to the gates of Fort Aguada, passing the guards on duty there. Abel had signed the roster, and he had pretended to sign it too. The guard in charge hadn't suspected anything. Abel had led him to the military parking-lot where he kept his motorcycle. On this they had sped away.

They had arrived in Margão just before dawn, when the town was deserted. As soon as Abel had parked his motorcycle near the town hall, he had seen a woman approaching them. Soon, she was hugging Abel who introduced him to Serafina Barbosa, his sweetheart and told him they were going to elope and that he, Mario, was coming with them across the Indian border, to be their interpreter, since he spoke both English and Hindi. Abel had told him he was sure that they would be treated well. They were going to Polem in the south of Goa, and from there across the border. However, before they could leave Margão, he had heard gunshot and seen Abel fall to the ground. Mario had been stunned. Serafina was crying hysterically, "You... Brute! Why Arnaldo? Why?"

"Serafina! Serafina!" the man had sobbed, the gun still in his hand. "I love you! I love you! Have you forgotten, my sister? Have you?"

"Sister...?" Mario began to understand.

Then Abel, in his dying moments, persuaded Mario to get away from the scene before the police arrived and escape to the Indian Union. Saying goodbye to Abel and Serafina he had gone to the railway station at Margão and boarded a train for the Indian Union. At Colem, the Portuguese custom post, he had got out and walked up and down the platform. In his uniform, no one had bothered him. He had boarded the train again when it was about to leave. At Castle Rock, he had got off the train, and as they knew, gone to the Indian police station, and surrendered himself.

This story sounded so unlikely to the Indian police that they suspected Mario was a Portuguese spy. When they heard *Emissora de Goa* denouncing him, there wasn't any doubt left in their minds. He had been sent into India to set up a network of spies, to replace one which the Indian police had recently uncovered in Bombay.

However, further investigations convinced them that Mario wasn't a Portuguese spy but a genuine nationalist. He had taken part in protest marches and had written an article exposing the lewd behaviour of the Portuguese troops. His imprisonment for rape, the Indian police now thought, was clearly intended to discredit him. When reports confirmed his escape from Fort Auguada and his daring killing of a Portuguese soldier, Mario was released as a hero.

Indian newspapers and radio stations pursued him for interviews, and though he told the story of his escape as truthfully as he could, it was so twisted and embroidered that Mario could not recognise the hero of these stories as himself.

The Goan political parties in the Indian Union – and there were many – the National Congress of Goa, United Front of Goans, Azad Gomantak Dal, Goan Peoples Party and others, all rushed to recruit him to boost their sagging morale. Mario saw now how the Goan political parties in India functioned. They fought with each other about who would lead the liberation, and competed for Nehru's approval, without whose blessing they would not undertake any political activity. Even when Nehru's policies hurt Goans, they would never dream of challenging him, particularly over the blockade. Mario had always thought that the liberation of Goa would be a farce without the support of the Goan people and what he saw of the Goan parties in India convinced him of this. They were only too ready to sell out Goan nationalism to the interests of their Indian political masters. Mario knew he would never join any of these parties.

CHAPTER XXV

Whilst he was still held in the Castle Rock police compound, Mario was visited by a Goan who seemed very different from those politicians who were so supine to Indian interests. This was Heriques Mendes; he had been campaigning ceaselessly to persuade the Indian Government to lift the blockade. He worked on behalf of Goans who had crossed into India illegally and were threatened with deportation. He challenged these deportations in the courts and sometimes won.

"I've a proposition for you," he said to Mario, on the day of his release. "I need a young man like you to assist me. You could come and stay with me."

Since he too opposed the blockade, and had nowhere else to go, Mario accepted Heriques' offer.

At his house, Heriques introduced his wife, Anna. Mario shook hands with her and smiled, but sensed that there was some awkwardness in the situation. This became evident when Rosita, their three year old daughter, came into the room. Without excusing herself, Anna left the room with the child. Heriques, too, was evidently uncomfortable. Later, when Mario saw Rosita again, he guessed what the embarrassment was: Rosita was a *mistiça*.

Heriques had no time for his family. He was always on the move, one day in Belgaum, the next in Bombay, helping Goans in distress. Mario wasn't idle either. Every day he would go to the police station to help Goans who had crossed the border and been detained. It was his job to hire lawyers to fight their cases and attend to Heriques' correspondence.

When Heriques was at home, his political friends would drop in on him. Their talk was all politics: Goan, Indian and international. Heriques had views on everything. He said, "Foreign aid will never help India."

"Why?" one of his friends asked.

"Though foreign aid is called aid without strings, it will drain India."

"How?"

"No dominant nation gives something for nothing. India's economic dependency will be deepened."

"You're voicing the views of Indian Communists such as Mr. Dange and Mr. Namoodripad."

"Maybe. I think they are right."

"Nehru is a wizard," another said. "He gets aid from both the U.S.A. and U.S.S.R."

"Wizard!" A sarcastic smile broke on Heriques' face.

"We can at least talk here," said one of the debaters. " It isn't like Goa."

"Without social justice," Heriques said, "democracy becomes the privilege of the few. The National Congress of India is an elite club and when the myth of Nehru and Mahatma Gandhi dies, and the people of India awaken, the National Congress of India will shatter like glass dropped from a height."

"Never! You're a dreamer!"

They would argue into the night and Mario, tired, would retire to his bed long before the debates ended.

One morning, while he was busy answering Heriques' correspondence, Anna came and stood by his desk and said abruptly, "You people think you can change the world."

Mario smiled and said, "There's no harm in trying."

"You people talk day in and day out about politics. What a waste of time!"

"Maybe it is," said Mario. "But your husband doesn't just talk, he's working to lift the blockade because he loves Goans."

"Love?" she said. "Or does he do all this for his ego?"

Mario looked at her, surprised.

"If he loves people, why can't he love his wife?" she said and ran out to her room.

Mario followed her and hesitantly knocked on her door. "Can I come in?"

"What do you want?"

She was sitting on the edge of her bed, her face in her hands, sobbing. He stood there wanting to say something consoling. But she was so distraught that he was drawn to sit by her side, and put his hand on her shoulder. She still sobbed. She rested her head on his chest, her body quaking. His heart beat faster. Gradually she stopped shaking, touched by Mario's gentleness, though she sensed his gaze

was fixed on something beyond and not on her. She brought his face
closer to hers and kissed him on the lips. When Mario realised what
had happened, he drew back and said, "I'm sorry."

She withdrew and said sharply, "I'm not a whore!"

"Who said you were!"

"Then, why did you..."

She gave Mario no chance to explain himself. "I was raped! I was
raped! I didn't let the paclo sleep with me, I didn't!"

"I know you didn't," Mario said trying to comfort her.

"I'm not a slut! I'm not a slut!"

"I think the very opposite of that."

More calmly she said, "Rosita is the product of that rape."

Between sobs, she told Mario what had happened.

It was her wedding day. Her bridal gown was white and very
beautiful. She looked so pretty that Heriques couldn't take his eyes
off her. He looked handsome too, very elegant, dressed in a black suit
and white gloves. The wedding reception was at Heriques' place at
sundown. After the church ceremony, the bridal party had stayed at
Heriques' godfather's place, before coming to bridegrooms' house.

"It was a happy moment," she said. "But the present is bitter and
the future won't be better."

"Things will get better," said Mario, wanting to comfort her.

She continued with the story. At sundown, to the accompaniment
of firecrackers, the bridal party had arrived at Heriques' house.
There Heriques' mother had anointed them with frankincense and
put the cordão, the family heirloom around Anna's neck. Then, the
ladainha started and when it was over, the guests were invited to see
her trousseau. Besides the gifts, her embroidery work and her high
school certificates were on display. The guests had admired her
achievements and praised her talents. There had been a quarrel
between her father and her mother-in-law over a Singer sewing
machine promised but not given by her father. But the dispute was
settled and family harmony restored.

After this there was the matov. Heriques took her in his arms and
with the band playing they had waltzed. She confessed that at that
moment she could hardly wait for the guests to go home so that she
and Heriques could retire to their matrimonial bed. Heriques' friends
had danced with her, the band had stopped playing; and a huge five-
tier cake coated in white, with a statuette of the bridal couple on the
top, had been brought into the matov. Champagne bottles popped and

glasses were raised to toast the bride and groom. Then she'd heard shouting. There was panic and she had felt Heriques' body start shaking and the champagne glass he was holding fell to the ground and broke. The military police had stormed in and she had passed out. It was only afterwards that she was told Heriques had been arrested.

"Why?" Mario asked.

"They said he had pasted up posters denouncing the Portuguese."

For a long time she hadn't known where Heriques was or what had happened to him. She would have gone insane if it hadn't been for her mother-in-law who'd been very kind to her. Then one afternoon, there'd been a pounding at the door. She'd been alone and terrified to see a man called Abreu Gama with two Portuguese soldiers. They claimed that Heriques had escaped from prison and that they'd come to search the house. She had sensed, though, that Abreu hadn't come for Heriques but for her.

"Who was this Abreu Gama?" Mario asked.

Anna explained that he was a government spy, hated in the village. He had used his power to extract money from the villagers, and demand sex from the village girls and married women. He'd made sexual advances to Anna, but had been firmly rebuffed. In the end, he'd even proposed to her, but she had rejected him, to his fury. He had asked her father to force Anna to marry him. Her father had refused. She had thought that once she'd married Heriques, he would forget about her. But now she had nowhere to escape, and though she'd bitten him, he'd overpowered her and stripped her with the help of the paclo soldiers. Her humiliation was not over though, for Gama had been unable to get an erection, though he pretended to take her. Then he had ordered the pacles to mount her in turn, which they did with great brutality. She had been, of course, still a virgin and her mother-in-law had come home to find her bruised and bleeding, but she was so ashamed that she had persuaded her not to go to the doctor.

A few days later, Heriques, who had indeed escaped from prison, came to the house late at night. He had woken her, taken her in his arms and kissed her. When he started to make love to her, she had thought about telling him of the rape, but had decided not to.

Two days later, they had escaped from Goa to India. With the help of Heriques' friends and money his mother had given him, they had settled in Castle Rock. Anna was happy, and when Heriques started to help the Goan emigrants, she had thrown herself into his work. But things had begun to change when she discovered she was pregnant.

She had been terrified, not knowing whose child she was carrying, and often woke up at nights sweating in panic. Heriques had been so loving, he would take her in his arms and do his best to calm her. She had wanted to tell him, but didn't have the courage, and hoped that the child in her womb would be his.

"But as you know, the child wasn't his."

"How did he react?"

There had been no reaction. If he had shouted at her or condemned her, she could have taken it. His silence, his indifference, hurt her as nothing had hurt her before. She shed tears and made scenes. Nothing moved him. He became engrossed in his work. Emotionally and physically he went away from her and she had become bitter towards his work.

Mario was ashamed to discover that her story had excited him. His hands were drawn to her blouse, caressing her breasts. She had unbuttoned his shirt and begun kissing his chest. Before he knew what was happening, she had let him undress her and before he could stop himself they were together in her bed, making love.

CHAPTER XXVI

That night, back in his own bed, a voice in his head rebuked him, "You're scum, you're nothing but scum!"

"But ..."

"But, what? You want to defend yourself?"

"But... I love her."

"Love? What do you know? You do remember Nirmala, don't you?"

Yet again he saw the flames swallowing up her body. He would dash towards the flames, but they threw him back. He was unclean.

"You're loathsome. Heriques brought you under his roof when you had nowhere to go. He gave you food, shelter and work. And how do repay him? You slept with his wife, didn't you? You're evil!"

"I'm not! I'm not!"

One night, hearing Mario call out in his sleep, Anna came into his bedroom. He was sobbing. She lay by his side. The night was silent and the room was dark. She wrapped her arms around him and kissed him gently. Mario awoke.

"Am I evil?" he asked.

"Evil? Why?"

"I'd no right to make love to you."

"Is it because you don't love me?"

Silence.

"Do you love me? Do you have feelings for me?" Her fingers like fishes in water swam all over his body, exploring him. She caressed his penis with loving tenderness. He caressed her breasts and stroked the cleft between her thighs. This time no voice came to torment him as they made love.

Afterwards, she said, "Thank you coming into my life."

After a long silence, he said, "But this is wrong."

"Wrong?"

"Yes," he said. "It is adultery."

"Is that what's bothering you? It shouldn't. Heriques did nothing to ease my pain. He deserted me like a leper. I knelt before him and begged to take me in his arms. He wouldn't. You brought love to me. We did nothing wrong."

"But there's another woman in my life, too," he said. "She came before you. I still love her and I love you. What can I do?"

"Another woman? Who's she?"

"Nirmala."

"But you told us she's dead. How can you betray her? She can't hold you as I can."

"I see her in my dreams."

"Of course you do! You'll always love her, but you must stop tormenting yourself. Perhaps her spirit brought us together."

"What do you mean?"

"Seeing our sufferings, she must have opened your heart to mine."

"But what about Heriques? I feel guilty. I've cuckolded him."

"Why go into all that? I've told you how little he feels for me." That night Mario slept peacefully.

He was still dozing when he heard a knocking at his door.

"Who's there?"

"It's me, Heriques."

When Mario opened the door, Heriques stood there smiling.

"I've good news," he said. "Our plans to protest against the blockade are going well. We're going by the evening train to Belgaum where we'll meet some of our supporters. Then we'll go on to Bombay. It's there we'll hold our biggest protest meeting yet. I need you to come with me, Mario."

When they were eating breakfast, Heriques told Anna, "Mario won't be at home tonight. In fact, both of us will be away, I don't know for how long."

As usual, she didn't make any comment.

When Heriques' friends came to see him, he told them about the protest meeting. The blockade would be lifted, he said, by the efforts of the Goans in India, and that would be the first lesson for Goans in democracy. While this talk was going on, Mario's mind was far away. He was hearing the voice again, perhaps not so close, but still insistent.

Anna had packed Heriques' suitcase. A pang of jealousy stabbed Mario. She was Heriques' wife, after all. Who was he? He heard the voice, "Stay away from them! You don't understand what they have." Later, when they were about to leave for the train, and Heriques said with concern, "Take care of yourself, Anna. I'll be home as soon as I can", Mario saw sparks of love between them. Jealousy and guilt struck him in equal proportions.

CHAPTER XXVII

Mario was daydreaming about Anna. She was dressed in a red sari, a flimsy silky material through which he could glimpse her breasts. A smile flickered on her lips. She approached him and the sari slithered from her body, very gracefully.

"Mario!" Heriques was sitting opposite him on the train.

But Mario was elsewhere.

"Mario!" he called again, shaking him by the knee.

Seeing Heriques' concerned face before him, Mario blushed deep scarlet.

"What's wrong with you, Mario? Do you have a fever?"

Mario's eyes welled with tears and he broke into sobs. Heriques was touched. He knew that prison did strange things to people. Though he was safe in India, he would often see Casmiro Monteiro, the head of PIDE, torturing him brutally, in his dreams.

"I went through hell myself," Heriques said. "I know what it is to be in a Portuguese prison. If it weren't for Anna, I would have never made it."

Mario was still sobbing and Heriques reached out to Mario and put his hand on his.

"I was hurt, very hurt..."

Though Mario stopped sobbing, he was very uncomfortable within. Did Heriques know?

"I was so pained when I knew Rosita wasn't my child," Heriques said softly and as the train went on he poured out the pain he had locked up for many years. He was so humiliated that his firstborn wasn't his, not even Goan, but a firngo's child. He had treated Anna so badly. He'd been indifferent to her, he'd called her all sorts of names; she'd kept quiet, as if she deserved them all. What bothered him most was the fear that Goans would laugh at him. Whenever he looked at Anna, he saw firngo soldiers ripping off her clothes and mounting her. He couldn't touch her.

"But just recently, I've started to see her again as I once did. I see something beautiful in her, something that's come alive again. But I'm so afraid to touch her. I was a fool, wasn't I? If only... I must ask her to forgive me," he said, looking at Mario. "Do you think she will?"

"I'm sure she will."

The train went on. Heriques was deep in thought. Mario looked through the window. He loved Nirmala but had never had sex with her. He loved Anna, the first woman to give him the joys of sex. Now, she would go to her husband.

Arriving late at night in Belgaum, they were welcomed by Sardinha Miranda, a friend of Heriques, who lived on High Street, Camp. Mario went straight to bed while Heriques and Sardinha talked about the economic blockade.

In the morning, when Mario came down for breakfast, he found Heriques and Sardinha talking about Edmundo Barbosa, one of the exiled Goan leaders who had begun to take a more independent position and was opposed to the blockade. Mario gathered that Barbosa was expected at the house that morning.

Hardly had they had sat down for breakfast when Barbosa arrived.

"Glad to see you," said Sardinha. "Heriques was getting worried. Want to eat some breakfast?"

"Thanks," said Barbosa." We had our breakfast on the way. Who's this young man?"

Mario was introduced and he and Barbosa shook hands.

Barbosa was in his thirties, a fair-skinned man who wore thick glasses on his nose – a fitting symbol of his scholastic achievement. He had read philosophy at an American university and was now a professor at the University of Karnataka. During his student days in India, he had taken part in the Civil Disobedience Movement and was a member of the Congress Party. He was a protégé of the Chief Minister of the State of Karnataka. Karnataka and Maharashtra, who had feuded over border and language issues, both had an eye on Goa. Fearing that Goa, once free from Portuguese rule, might be annexed by Maharashtra, the Chief Minister of Karnataka had asked Barbosa to support Heriques in his attempt to remove the Indian economic blockade. So Barbosa had come to Belgaum, with his entourage of Goan students from the Karnataka University, to help promote the opposition to the blockade.

Mario went with these students from house to house among the Goans in Belgaum.

"India is a secular republic," they would argue. "Goans shouldn't be afraid to express their opinions in India. The blockade hurts ordinary Goans the most and it should be lifted."

The Goans of Belgaum were impressed by this new breed of Goan youth – bold and fearless, molded by Indian democracy. The young were well drilled by Barbosa, and in every house they visited, they repeated the same arguments parrot-fashion. Even some of the eminent Goans in Belgaum who had kept aloof from the Liberation Movement gave press-statements supporting Barbosa.

When the protest meeting was held, the Goans of Belgaum came in droves, demanding the removal of the blockade. At the end of his address, Barbosa shouted, "Goa for the Goans! Goa for the Goans!"

And the auditorium reverberated with the cry.

CHAPTER XXVIII

After their successful meeting in Belgaum, Barbosa and Heriques worked on the plans for their campaign in Bombay. Barbosa, who had high hopes of becoming the first Chief Minister of liberated Goa, left nothing to chance. He sent ahead his student deputy, Joe Gonsalves, to prepare the ground. Heriques dispatched Mario to go along with Joe.

On the train to Bombay, Mario learnt much about the realities of their movement.

"Edmundo Barbosa is the right person to be leader," said Joe. "Like Nehru, he is a brahmin. Doesn't matter that he's Catholic. He comes from a traditional fidalgo family in Goa, so he's like a bat in the fable, a bird and a mammal."

"I don't understand."

"The Indian National Congress sees that he can be put to use for their benefit. The Hindu and Catholic brahmins in Goa trust him too. Nehru wants to free Goa without firing a shot. If Barbosa can deliver that, Nehru has a chance to win the Nobel Prize for Peace. And you know how much he wants that! The other Goan parties here can't free Goa, they're just barking dogs. You don't understand the scheming behind Goan politics, Mario. Barbosa is wooed by all the parties. He's a shrewd Ibero-Brahmin. He's convinced the elites in Goa that if India invades Goa, the power won't be in their hands. So the eminent sons of Goa, and there's one eminent daughter, too, have signed up for autonomous status for Goa. I tell you, he'll be the first Chief Minister of Goa, though the other Goan politicians here don't like him."

In Bombay, Mario and Joe went straight to work. They visited the *kuds*, the village clubs in the Goan ghettoes, where mainly male immigrants lived. Mario found out that even these were based on caste. They visited kud after kud, and Joe hammered home the message that India was a secular democratic state and Goans in Bombay shouldn't fear to speak against the blockade. The Bombay Goans were as receptive as those in Belgaum.

Barbosa and Heriques arrived a few days before the meeting.
Barbosa, dressed in homespun cloth and wearing his Gandhi cap,
went with Mario and Joe to the kuds. He wouldn't be forgotten when
it came to the elections after Goa's liberation.

Though there was some coverage of Barbosa's activities, he felt
there wasn't enough, so he called a press conference two days before
the meeting and spoke boldly against the blockade. The Goans in the
kuds were impressed. They said he didn't spare Nehru, that he'd
come down hard on him and asked him to remove the blockade on
humanitarian grounds. Even *Ave Maria*, the Konkani daily of
Bombay, a pro-Portuguese paper, described Barbosa as a rare breed
of a leader, bold and fearless; he was the leader Goans were waiting
for. Barbosa read and reread this article; yes, yes, he was getting
closer to his goal. What a tickling sensation that was!

Mario's political education continued when, one evening, Barbosa
invited him and Heriques to visit a friend on Malabar Hill.

"He's very interested in you, Mario," Barbosa said. "He's
impressed with what he has read about you. He thinks, you ..." his
voice trailed off.

By then, the taxi had stopped outside a palatial mansion. Mario
looked down on the city. From above, the lights looked beautiful and
none of the repulsive city smells reached Malabar Hill. The security
guard was already checking their identities and soon a man in his
thirties, dressed in homespun cloth, with his hands clasped over his
bulging belly, came out to welcome them.

"This is Ashok Patel," said Barbosa introducing their host. I n
the living room, Mario felt that he was Ali Baba in cave full of riches.
It was cool and comfortable. On the wall, besides paintings from the
Mogul period, Mario's eyes were drawn to a framed group photograph.
Ashok, observing Mario's curiosity, led him to the photograph.

"That's my uncle." Ashok pointed to a man wearing the familiar
homespun uniform and Gandhi cap. The camera had caught the
dawning of a smile. Nehru and other bigwigs of the National
Congress were there in the photograph. Ashok thought a small
history lecture would be in good taste, especially when the hero of
the history happened to be his uncle.

"My uncle," he said, "sacrificed a lot for this country. Edmundo
knew my uncle and my uncle regarded him as a son."

"He was a fine man," said Barbosa, his eyes smiling behind his
glasses.

"He has been, God knows how many times, in and out of British jails. He loved the people and was devoted to the Mahatma. Because of his Gandhian modesty, he never sought the limelight. He worked patiently and quietly behind the scenes."

"He was a very pragmatic man," said Barbosa. "A true interpreter of Gandhian ideology, but above all, he was a bridge between the business community and the common people. He knew how to sell the Mahatma to rich and poor alike."

"Yes," said Ashok. "He was a *brahamacharya*, he never married. His whole life was a service to the nation. And this is the reason why..."

"Ashok is blessed," said Barbosa, finishing what Ashok wanted to say.

Ashok smiled gracefully.

The conversation continued. Mario gathered that Ashok's father, a businessman, had done well out of his brother's political connections.

"When I came back home from the States," said Ashok, "my mind throbbed with new business ideas, which I wanted to put into action. But it wasn't easy..."

"Why was that?" Heriques asked.

"You know, how fathers are," said Ashok. "He was set in his ways about how to run the business. But, he was widowed and getting old. He wanted me married. He said, 'I'll hand you over the business anytime, provided you get married.' And now..."

And now, Ashok Patel was married to a girl of his own caste, the daughter of a powerful politician. With such connections, he had his fingers in many pies.

"Edmundo, I know your drink, what about your friends?" Ashok asked.

This came as a shock to Mario, in prohibition-bound Bombay. The Gandhian Ashok had an array of drinks. He had Scotch whisky, French cognac, Portuguese maceira and Portuguese wines – all smuggled from Goa.

He poured measures of Johnny Walker for Barbosa and Heriques, but into his own glass he poured a generous portion of Royal Salute – "The only whisky I drink."

"What about you Mario?"

"A beer."

They all toasted the success of the next day's protest meeting, Ashok gulping his whisky neat.

Over the drinks, Ashok told Barbosa that Sundrabai Hall had been booked and paid for; everything had been set for the meeting. "Do you need any more money?" he asked. But without waiting for Barbosa's answer, he put a bundle of rupee-notes into his hand.

Before offering to take them back to their respective hotels, Ashok said, "You have a big future, Mario. We'll back your political career. Are you a member of the National Congress?"

"Not yet," Mario answered.

"There isn't a better party than the National Congress. Never forget that. The National Congress drove the British away from India; and they'll drive the Portuguese, too. Be patient!"

That night, in his dreams, Mario saw a pack of white hounds with sharp teeth and seraphic smiles. One among them, the leader of the pack barked as if giving a speech, while the others sheepishly listened to it.

CHAPTER XXIX

Sunderabai Hall was packed. On the podium, flanked by the main speakers, Edmundo Barbosa sat beaming behind his spectacles. He got up and came to the microphone. Clad in spotless homespun white with a Gandhi cap on his head, he looked at the audience before him. He wanted to read their minds. He began his oration in Konkani — slow, loud and clear. Though his Konkani was rather peculiar, it didn't matter. The audience knew that he was a foreign-educated Goan but enough of a man of the people to use their tongue and they were proud of him. He enumerated yet again the reasons why the blockade should be lifted.

Heriques spoke in the same vein, and after him came a succession of speakers all pleading with Nehru to lift the blockade. The audience applauded, though increasingly politely.

But when Simon Rodrigues came to the microphone, a short corpulent man in his fifties, dressed in spotless white trousers and white turtleneck coat, there was quite a stir among the audience. They had known him as the ex-mayor of Bombay and as a Konkani scholar who had translated some of Shakespeare's plays. Though Rodrigues had kept away from politics up to this point, Barbosa had managed to lure him to his cause. He delivered his discourse like a pulpit-pounding preacher. His voice boomed in the hall and his hand gestures mesmerised the audience. When he had finished speaking, the audience applauded nonstop, giving him a standing ovation. There wasn't anything new in what he said, but the force of his utterance had captured them.

Barbosa and Heriques entreated Mario to speak. He came to the microphone and looked at the audience as if he were frozen with fear. He saw the white hounds stripping the flesh from these people. Then this mirage melted away and he spoke.

"Our leaders have spoken," he said. "They have all made very eloquent speeches, asking the benevolent Prime Minister of India to lift the blockade. But none of them told you what action they would take if the benevolent Prime Minister of India didn't listen to their pleas." Here he paused and looked around at Barbosa, Heriques, Simon and the others on the podium. Turning back to the audience he said, "If we want the blockade to end, we must decide what action we will take if the benevolent Prime Minister of India doesn't listen to our request. Injustice, wherever it is, must be rooted out and replaced by justice."

"Fight the injustice in Goa first!" someone from the audience shouted. "Don't come here and talk about injustice. Don't abuse Indian democracy!"

"You're very right!" Mario said to the heckler.

"Of course, I am!"

"What action do you propose to throw out Portuguese colonialism?" Mario asked him.

"We Goans from India should march into Goa and claim our motherland," answered the heckler.

"Would you lead us?" asked Mario.

There was no response from the heckler and Mario repeated his question.

"Leave him alone," somebody else from the audience shouted. "We haven't come here to free Goa from Portuguese rule. This meeting is about the blockade."

"Yes, yes, yes," the audience went on shouting.

When the clamour had died, Mario turned towards Barbosa and demanded, "What plans do you have, if the Prime Minister of India doesn't listen to your plea?"

The Gandhian smile behind Barbosa's spectacles had gone. Casting a pained look at Mario, he approached the microphone and pleaded with the audience to calm down. "To be honest with you," he said, "and honesty being my policy, we haven't made any plans because we are confident that Mr. Nehru, who is well known for his humanitarianism, will listen to our pleas."

"Has the Indian Government asked you to hold this meeting to save its face?" a tall man from the audience asked. Barbosa remained silent. The man continued, "This economic blockade is inhuman. Many nations of the world disapprove of it. It's a blot on Nehru's reputation. How much money have they given you to arrange this protest meeting and get Nehru off the hook? How much Barbosa? How much?"

"How much! How much!" the audience chanted nonstop; and Barbosa couldn't calm them down.

"Keep quiet! Keep quiet!" shouted the tall man. "The saviour of the Goans wants to say something."

The audience roared with laughter. Then someone threw a rotten egg; it landed on Barbosa's spectacles, spreading its yolk. A volley of rotten eggs, tomatoes, rocks and soda bottles flew towards the podium. As the speakers were escaping the pandemonium, some jeered loudly, "Barbosa don't use the Goan people to further your political career! Let this be a lesson to you, Barbosa!"

Next day, Barbosa called his disciples to his room at the Ambassador Hotel. Mario was summoned. When he arrived, Barbosa demanded, "What right did you have to disrupt the meeting?"

"I didn't," he said. "I think the audience had the right to know your plans if the Indian Government didn't lift the blockade."

"You had no right to sabotage the campaign like that. Either you are not what we took you to be or you're more naïve than I can credit. You don't understand even the ABCs of politics!"

"I understand politics, Mr. Barbosa," said Mario. "From what I've seen in Bombay, I think I know how politics works here; and it stinks."

"It stinks?"

"Yes; it does!" said Mario. "You don't want the masses to be liberated; you want them to be passive and to accept you without challenge. Isn't it that so? Leaders like you make the masses promises, but never fulfil them and leave them in the gutters and the slums; that's democracy for you, isn't it? You're nothing but a bunch of hypocrites. You can preach Gandhi, you can preach Buddha and you can preach Christ, but none of you want to act according to the principles of these masters."

"Rome wasn't built in a day; one must be patient," Barbosa said wearily. "In due course poverty in India will be eliminated. Democracy and socialistic economic policies are the only way to free India from poverty."

"Democracy without the elimination of poverty is the democracy of the wealthy few," Mario retorted. "The Indian masses are voting fodder to bring these wealthy few to power; the wealthy few make promises, play upon caste, language and religious loyalties and get elected. Once they are in the legislature what do they do to eliminate poverty? Drink Dimple and Royal Salute whiskies? Live in big mansions and sleep in luxury hotels with their mistresses? These are the people who have inherited India from the British. They preach Gandhian doctrines and spout socialistic slogans while the Indian masses sleep in the gutters!"

Getting no response from Barbosa, Mario spoke again, "Mr. Barbosa, I saw Ashok Patel giving you a bundle of rupees in notes. That was black money, wasn't it?"

Everybody in India knew the role of the black money, money made illegally. There were many ways of doing it – foreign exchange transactions, bribes, kickbacks and host of other ways. Indian politicians used black money at election time to buy votes.

"You're naive," said Barbosa finally, "you'll never be a politician; in fact, you'll be nothing."

"I don't want to be a politician," said Mario. "But you have everything that can make you our Goan Nehru."

"What do you mean?" asked one of Barbosa's disciples.

"When Barbosa begins his political speeches, he can start in Konkani: *Mujea mogal bhavando anic bhonido*. The audience will explode in applause; and then he can render the same words in Portuguese in authentic Lisboa or Coimbra accent: *Meus senhores and minhas senhoras*. The lusotropicales and their sons and daughters will explode with joy, feeling that Portugal has not quite left Goa for good. And then, with Oxford or Cambridge accent, he will say the same words in English: *Ladies and gentlemen*. The anglicised Goans will applaud him with exuberance, wanting their sons and daughters to be like him. All he needs to do is conclude his speeches by shouting *Jai Goa! Jhai Hind!* Then he'll have covered every option. If he plays his cards well, he's sure to be elected. But what does he stand for? I want to see a free Goa, but one based on justice and equality."

With that, Mario stormed out of the room.

CHAPTER XXX

Mario took a bus ride through the city after he had left Barbosa's place. He sat on the upper deck, looking at the crowds. Not so many years ago he'd been at Bombi's restaurant in his village, listening to Nehru's speech on India's independence on the radio. He'd been full of hope that a new era would dawn in India. What India got was politicians who simply mimicked the political styles of their former colonial bosses, Gandhian in appearance but rapacious in substance. This wasn't the place to preach his paradise. He had to go back to Goa. He missed Goa. The very sounds and smells of his village came wafting to him, and he heard his mother calling, "Mario come home! Come home!"

He saw the faces of Cursin, Hut João, Mud Bosteão, Tar Menin, Plough Francis, Oji-mai Concentin, Modo-mai Majakin, senhor Tolentinho and others. He knew their pettiness, their greed, their joys and sorrows, but they were still the beads of his godmother's rosary. He had to go back.

He went to Victoria Railway Station and bought a ticket to Castle Rock. From there, he would walk down through the mountains to Goa. He got a seat in a crowded third-class compartment. Tired, he soon fell asleep. He dreamt his mother was in the back yard calling for the pig. "*Gheo! Gheo!*" She was fattening it to be butchered for the banquet that she would be giving for his homecoming.

The train reached Castle Rock early the following morning. Anna's house was not far away. He wondered about her just one more time, but he resisted the temptation; instead, he went to a store and bought some loaves and fruits and set off for the border.

He wandered his way down the Ghats. He felt free. Through thicket and bush he walked, listening to the birds singing. He had felt the same joy when he was young, sitting by the River Sal and listening to the songs of toddy-tapper Inas. When the sun was overhead, he sat under the shade of a tree and took a loaf from his bag, and sank his teeth into it.

As he was eating, he heard movements in the branches above. Looking up, he saw a monkey jeering at him. He offered it a banana, placing one on the ground. Hesitantly it came down from the tree and, squatting a few yards away, ate its meal with him, looking at him with sad eyes. Soon after, he saw a deer coming out of a thicket followed by a fawn. The deer looked at him too for quite a while without stirring, before disappearing into the trees.

His eyes felt heavy so he lay down to sleep on fallen leaves under the tree. When he awoke, the sun was no longer overhead and he continued on his way. Soon, he realised, the sun would be going down. Everything was bathed in its translucent glow. It was very peaceful. Then, as his path went close to a river bank, he stopped in his tracks, seeing a tiger lapping the water. The tiger lifted its head and looked at him. Mario shivered and froze. When he looked again, it was gone.

Now the sun had gone down and birds were quiet. Above, the stars twinkled and a yellow moon shimmered. Mario felt seized by a spiritual ecstasy and then an immense calm. What was there to fear in this world?

CHAPTER XXXI

It was early in the morning when he awoke. He did his toilet, ate the rest of the loaf and took to the road again, soon coming to the top of Dudsagor Falls. He was in Goa.

He sat at the top of the falls watching the cascading water and the yawning chasms of the Ghats with the blue forests below. He felt connected to something that was bigger even than the rosary beads of his village of Cavellosim

He walked down the mountain, hardly meeting anybody, except for a cowherd minding his cattle. On the road, a military jeep passed him. Arriving in the village of Sanaulim, he saw a bar, *Casa Portuguesa*. He was thirsty and felt like having a beer.

When Mario entered the bar, he found a couple of local men and a policeman drinking there. He sat at a table, looking around. On the wall was a framed photo of Dr. Salazar and a cloth banner embossed with a slogan: AQUI É PORTUGAL. Then Mario saw his own portrait, not framed, but pasted on the wall, labelled: WANTED CRIMINAL.

Mario went to the counter and ordered a beer. He drank it in great gulps and ordered another which he downed even more quickly. He ordered yet another. This one he drank slowly. He ought to be going home to his mother. But when he got there, he reflected, the Regedor would come and arrest him. Seeing his glass empty, he ordered another beer.

He studied his portrait on the wall and grinned. In the not-too-distant future Salazar's portrait would come down. Maybe he would become the first chief minister of liberated Goa, and not Barbosa. He imagined himself in that position, the applause of the people ringing in his ears. There instead of Salazar's portrait would be his, hanging in gold frames in public places. Schools and academies would be named after him and the school children would call him Tio-Mario or Chacha-Mario.

Sipping his beer, he thought about Anna, the first woman with whom he'd had sex. She was the woman to share his life, and thinking about her, he was aroused. He would have to marry someone else to give respectability to his position, but he would take Anna as his mistress, and, of course, make her husband Heriques a minister.

He ordered more beer. The bartender looked at him quizzically.

Then the thought came: Why shouldn't he be the prime minister of India? They were already asking, After Nehru who? A Catholic prime minister in Hindu India!

He saw himself dressed in Nehru fashion – a long white coat, white jodhpur-like pants and a Gandhi cap on his head, standing tall and erect before the Indian multitude. Filled with power and glory, he began, "Bhaino! Behono!" and ended, "Jhai Hind! Jhai Hind!"

He grinned from ear to ear, sipping more beer. He wouldn't make empty promises, make black money white, nor black-marketeers honest men. He would hang them from the nearest tree. He would be revered not only in his country but throughout the world. But there was no more beer in his glass. When he asked for more beer, the bartender said, "Pay for the ones you have drunk, than I'll open another one."

"Do you know who you are talking to?" Mario asked.

The bartender knew that with a little patience and flattery he could make the drunk pay for his drinks. He smiled.

"Do you see that portrait on the wall?" Mario asked.

"Who are you? I never saw you here before."

"I'm the Prime Minister!"

"Is that so? Well, Mr Prime Minister, I'm honoured that you came to my bar," said the bartender. "But since you're the Prime Minister, you should set a good example. Pay for your drinks, Mr Prime Minister."

"Of course! Here," he said, putting some rupees on the counter, "give me another beer."

"But these are rupees," said the bartender. "In here, we pay in escudos, you should have known that, Mr. Prime Minister."

"I don't have escudos," said Mario.

"No escudos? I don't care who you are!" said the bartender. "How is it that you're carrying the enemy's money?"

"Give me another beer!"

The bartender called over the policeman, and when he had come, Mario said to him, "You know who I am!"

"I know that you are Dr. Salazar," said the policeman.

"No! No!" said Mario. "I'm not Dr. Salazar. Don't insult me!"

"Who are you then?" asked the policeman.

"I'm the future chief minister of Goa! The next prime minister of India! I'm Mario!"

Who hadn't heard of Mario in Goa? Could this man really be Mario? The policeman looked at Mario's portrait on the wall; then he looked at Mario. He wasn't sure. But when the bartender looked at Mario's portrait, and then looked back at Mario again, he was certain and he cried, "You are Mario!"

The policeman was alarmed. Could this drunk really be Mario, the killer and terrorist? Many said he had demonic powers, that he could make himself invisible. Even the brave Portuguese soldiers were afraid of him. Otherwise, how could he have escaped from Fort Aguada? Only yesterday, *Emissora de Goa* had announced that Brigadier Chaves, hunting in the forest of Sanguem, had been shot dead in cold blood by Mario.

The policeman pointed his revolver unsteadily towards Mario. The thought crossed his mind that Mario might turn invisible, snatch his revolver and kill him. Secretly, he removed the bullets from his revolver.

"Give him another beer," the policeman told the bartender.

"But who is going to pay for all these beers?"

The policeman paid for the beers and Mario thanked him and asked, "What's your name?"

The policeman didn't answer Mario. What point was there in taking chances?

Since there wasn't a telephone in the bar, the policeman dispatched a messenger to the nearest police station informing them that he had arrested Mario at *Casa Portuguesa*.

A whole unit of police force arrived to find Mario still drinking his beer, with the policeman unsteadily pointing his revolver at him.

Mario continued to sip his beer and when they handcuffed him, he offered no resistance. As they were shoving him into the jeep to take him to Panjim Central Police Station, he looked at the policeman who had arrested him and asked him again, "What's your name?"

CHAPTER XXXII

Next day in the morning, after he was given breakfast, Mario was ushered into the presence of Casmiro Monteiro, the chief of PIDE, Chefe Vasquito and Capitão Braz Pinto. This unholy trinity looked at him and exchanged glances. Casmiro Monteiro looked hard at Mario and then nodded his head. The other two returned his nod, and when Mario was checked for fingerprints there wasn't any doubt left in their minds about who their captive was.

But why had he come back to Goa and allowed himself to be taken so easily? He could have barked from India like the rest of the Goan nationalists. Had he come to dynamite a bridge? Blow up a Government building?

"Why have you come back, Mario?" Monteiro asked.

Mario looked at him for a long time without answering.

Having gone through Mario's dossier, Monteiro knew that he sometimes had bouts of insanity. His village vicar had said that he had been possessed by evil spirits when young; that he had made himself drunk on church wine, had eaten consecrated wafers and proclaimed to the whole village that there wasn't a God. Even as he was being arrested, he had boasted that he was the future prime minister of India! Casmiro Monteiro was not a stupid man. It was all too clear that the man they had arrested was far from the super-hero of the popular imagination or the arch-villain of Portuguese propaganda. Nevertheless, they could still use Mario. His arrest was to be kept secret. The responsibility for any terrorist activity inside Goa could still be dumped on Mario.

For their part, the Goan nationalists accused PIDE of killing Mario. Lurid details of how he had been tortured to death appeared in the Indian newspapers. Mario, in the meantime, languished in his cell.

CHAPTER XXXIII

Whilst Mario remained in Panjim prison, the political imperatives on the Indian Government were changing. The first armed clash with China had taken place, and in the Parliament the Defence Minister, Krishna Menon, was being accused of not defending India's territorial integrity.

General elections were in the offing, and Nehru knew that the blame would not be confined to his defence minister. It was time to play the Goan card. He felt grateful to dictator Salazar for not conceding to his peaceful overtures. Now, with military might, he would invade Goa, uprooting Portuguese colonialism from Indian soil, once and for all. He and Menon would emerge as conquering heroes, the smashers of the oldest invader of Mother India and he would be re-elected when his term was up. Would it bother Nehru to violate Mahatma Gandhi's credo of nonviolence? Once virginity is lost, it's lost for good. The stage was set. In October 1961, an Afro-Asian seminar on Portuguese colonialism was held in New Delhi. The delegates voiced clearly their support of violence to end Portuguese colonialism. Nehru began to wonder at a public meeting in Bombay whether, "the time has come for us to consider afresh what method should be adopted to free Goa from Portuguese rule."

War hysteria was let loose. The Indian press and radio set out to convince the world that Portugal had concentrated a vast army in Goa and was threatening aggression on India. One day, Lakshmi Menon, Nehru's Deputy in the Ministry of External Affairs, peering from a safe place at Majali on the India-Goa border, was horrified to see with her telescopic eyes the brutalities inflicted on the innocent Goans. Convening a press conference, she declared that thousands of Goans had been arrested, and appealed to her Prime Minister for immediate armed intervention, though she wasn't sure if nonviolent Nehru would heed her pleas.

The Portuguese establishment, sensing the imminent danger, and knowing that their forces would be no match for India, asked Goans to pray to Saint Francis Xavier, their patron saint. If anybody could rescue them from the agnostic Nehru, Saint Francis would. He had come to Portugal's aid many times before, hadn't he?

The Governor General, Vassalo e Silva, went down on his knees and prayed that nonviolent Nehru wouldn't attack Goa. (Once, the same Governor had ordered Goans to pray for Nehru's health, and they had done just that. How ungrateful that agnostic Nehru was!)

As the tension mounted, more and more acts of sabotage occurred within Goa. The Portuguese Government was keen to put the blame for these events on the Indian Government rather than the internal opposition. With foreign journalists arriving in Goa, Casmiro Monteiro, the Chief of the PIDE, thought that it was now time to make use of Mario. He would give concrete evidence that India was committing aggression in Goa.

So, after almost three years in solitary confinement, Mario was taken from his cell and brought before Casmiro Monteiro.

"We'll do a little writing," said Monteiro.

Mario was made to sit at a desk and given paper and a pen.

Monteiro dictated, "I, Mario... hereby make a full confession of all my crimes..."

But Mario wasn't moving his pen.

"Write!" Monteiro bellowed.

He dictated again. Mario still didn't put pen to paper.

"You want to be tortured?" Monteiro asked. "If that's what you want, that's what you'll get."

Mario was beaten, yet he still wouldn't confess. Monteiro didn't give up. Mario was made to stand against a wall on his tiptoes for almost two days. Exhausted by this prolonged torture, Mario frequently collapsed on the floor, quivering, but still refused to sign. Monteiro looked at him and wondered. Was there really a demon in him?

Lying flat on the floor, still in convulsions, Mario imagined that he was defecating some of the future chief ministers and politicians of liberated Goa. They were massive lumps of putrid, stinking faeces. A fat one who had dropped through his anus had once been a pauper, had become a leading trafficker of smuggled goods, established his political connections and was now terrorising the people. Another who followed through Mario's anus was no better; a first class kleptocrat who was misusing Government funds and putting the money in foreign banks. This wasn't the Goa he once knew; it was a mountainous dungheap of politicians. Filled with revulsion, Mario shouted, "No! No!"

"No?" Monteiro shouted angrily, and kicked him hard.

"No! No!" Mario groaned, his paroxysms coming faster.

"No? You won't?" Monteiro raged, kicking him again.

When the seizures stopped, Mario lay on the floor calm and quiet. Now he was soaring upwards, how he wasn't sure. When he looked down he could see a blue valley with blue mountains, blue forests, rivers, springs and a blue sea. Coming down he saw a village of whitewashed houses with red roofs and flower-gardens at the front. There was a group of girls at the well, among them Nirmala. Now he was back on the ground and she turned her head. Seeing Mario, she blushed and the other girls giggled, as if they knew that he was her sweetheart. Casting furtive glances at him, she walked away with a water-pot on her hip. He walked on and saw Anna in the front of a whitewashed house. He stood there and looked at her with longing eyes. She saw him, looked at him for a few seconds and went into the house. It was still early morning; roosters were crowing. This was his village, – the notables and the serfs were the same – but here they seemed to mix without distinctions. He saw Jozin-Bab, the centenarian outside his house, weaving a palm-leaf into a mat. Jozin-Bab peered through his bifocals. Recognising Mario, he asked him to sit down.

When Mario had sat, he said, "Always remember this, Mario: A nation that doesn't aspire to be an industrial giant may be exploited by the others. But a nation that doesn't grow spiritually will be in worse trouble."

"I'll remember," answered Mario.

Weaving the palm-leaf, Jozin-Bab said, "Once, in my youth, I dreamt of black crows eating black crows. I know what it means now. Indians are eating Indians."

Mario, laid out like a cadaver on the floor, had an idiotic smile on his face. Monteiro was impatient. He kicked Mario as hard as he could, until Mario came back from his trance. He took out his penis and pissed on Mario's face and in desperation shouted, "If you don't sign the charge sheet, I'll shit on you!"

Reluctantly, Mario signed, fearing that Monteiro wouldn't hesitate to defile him in this way.

That same day, General Vassalo e Silva, the Governor of *Estado da India Portuguesa*, armed with the confession, called a press conference. Before the international and local journalists, the Governor declared that Mario Jaques, who had committed many acts of sabotage inside Goa, had finally been caught red-handed in an attempt to dynamite Mormugão's harbour installations. He read out Mario's admission that he had been paid to act on behalf of the Indian government.

The story and Mario's photograph appeared on the front pages of the Goan dailies. At last, they said, the WANTED CRIMINAL had been caught and they enumerated all his crimes and published his written confession with a photograph of his signature.

The Indian newspapers also displayed his photograph on their front pages, praising him as a hero, a true patriot, a true son of the soil. They claimed that Mario had been sadistically tortured to death and his body burned. How long, they asked, was India going to tolerate, in the name of nonviolence, the barbarities of Salazar's regime on the sacred soil of India? Nonviolence didn't mean cowardice or impotence. How could nonviolent India's conscience be at peace when dauntless nationalists like Mario and many others were being brutally murdered in Goa? Enough was enough.

Nonviolent Nehru couldn't take it any more. Embracing the new credo of nonviolent violence, India's troops marched into Goa on December 18, 1961. Indian jets roared across the Goan sky and the Indian navy sailed into Goan waters. Goans locked their doors and prayed to St. Francis Xavier, led by their kneeling Governor. He prayed to Afonso de Albuquerque, the conquistador who had conquered Goa for Portugal, but the Indian jets still roared in the sky, and none of these saints, not even Afonso de Albuquerque, stirred in their graves to come to their aid.

Portuguese soldiers, outnumbered, abandoned their guns and ran for their lives. In truth, they weren't soldiers but peasants conscripted from their villages to defend a crumbling empire. Within thirty-six hours, four-hundred-fifty-one years of Portuguese colonialism in Goa were over.

Goa had been liberated and though international opinion spluttered and Nehru was seen as a little less saintly, Congress won the elections.

BOOK IV

CHAPTER XXXIV

The Portuguese flag came down and the Indian flag fluttered victoriously in its place. The prisons were emptied of all prisoners, and Mario returned home to his mother.

With tear-filled eyes, Rosa saw Mario from the verandah. She ran to him, hugged him, kissed him and looked at him for a quite a while. But her motherly instinct told her that the old Mario had not come home. Later, after some days, she tried to coax him to settle down, marry and have children, but he only smiled gently, looking distant.

The villagers had mixed feelings about him. For some he was still the criminal of the defunct government's propaganda; for others he was a hero returned. But even those who blamed the collapse of the Portuguese regime on Mario's activities, who expected that he would brag about them as some nationalists were doing, were surprised that he did nothing of the kind.

Instead, at night, he would sit outside and gaze at the starry sky. Often, he would be there the whole night. Rosa was very concerned. Was he still possessed? When Hut João, his godfather and Neunita Figueiredo, his godmother, came to visit him, they left very soon after they had come, feeling uncomfortable in his presence.

"This liberation was forced upon us," remarked Thomas Rodrigues, visiting Mario at home one day. Rodrigues was from Cavelossim, and he claimed that Mario and Apolinario, the village teacher, had influenced him. When Apolinario was banished from the village and Mario sent to prison, Thomas had taken on the task of teaching the fisherfolk's children to read and write. But he too had been accused of preaching communism to the poor and thrown behind bars.

"Why do you say that?" Mario asked.

"Look at the Indian military Governor of Goa, Major General K.P. Candeth. He thinks he's Napoleon or a kind of Caesar and the Indian military look upon us as conquered people. What they don't understand is that Goan nationalism has its roots in Goan nativism. Between them, Dictator Salazar and nonviolent Nehru have robbed Goans of their independence. He robbed us of our right to free ourselves from Portuguese colonialism. In Portuguese times, our leaders ran to Lisbon, or Panjim to confer with the Governor; now, they will run to New Delhi and Goa will be sold to non-Goans by our leaders."

"This India will not build anything new," Mario said dully.

"Why not?"

Mario didn't respond and Thomas, looking at him, began to wonder what damage his old teacher had suffered.

Coming out of his trance at last, Mario said, "The only new thing, the concept of nonviolence – the very soul of India – that the Mahatma resuscitated in thousands of Indians and non-Indians has been destroyed; the very soul of India has been poisoned."

"What do you mean?"

"You know, Thomas," said Mario. "The Mahatma tried to purify his own soul before preaching nonviolence to the masses. It was a war between matter and spirit, and he won the war, defeated the temptations of the body and matter. Thousands of the downtrodden who came to him saw themselves mirrored in his soul, they understood him and he understood them. They came in droves to drive away British imperialism from Indian soil, not with violence, but with soul-force, nonviolence. Who will now drive away Indian imperialism from Indian soil?"

Thomas looked at Mario without responding.

"You know, Thomas," Mario continued, "true liberation and true independence are far off. A new breed of exploiters will come to liberated Goa, talk the language of freedom and even quote the Mahatma. They will take everything away from us."

As they were talking, they heard a woman lamenting loudly, as if for the loss of someone close to her. They recognised the voice of Agnela, Mario's next door neighbour. Then she came storming up to them.

"Mario-Bab, do you call this liberation?"

"What's wrong, Agnela?"

"They've taken away my husband! I curse them!"

"Your husband?"

"Yes, Mario-Bab, my husband. I'm married to Cicero Leite two years now. He's a paclo. They've rounded up all pacles, and have put them somewhere. Nobody knows where. They say they're going to kill them all. What am I supposed to do?"

A villager who had just joined them said, "Why are you moaning, Agnela? That paclo wasn't your husband, you're just his whore! Shut up and go home!"

Agnela cursed and called the man all sorts of names. When Mario intervened, trying to comfort her, she said, "You brought all this on us! Why did you hate the Portuguese? My Cicero was a good man, better than all of you!"

"What's going on here?" Rosa Jaques demanded.

"Ocobae," said Agnela, "My husband, Cicero Leite, is arrested by the Indian soldiers. They say they are going to kill him. When I went to look for him, no one tells me anything. Instead, drunken bearded soldiers make advances on me, wanting to... I ran away, Ocobae, I ran away!"

"Have patience, Agnela. They won't kill him."

"Who can trust these Indians!" Agnela cried out. "They said that Nehru was a nonviolent man; see now what he did! Indians don't keep the principles they preach. People like Mario-Bab brought them into Goa."

"Why are you blaming my son?"

"Why shouldn't I?" Agnela demanded. "Mario-Bab is one of those who drove the Portuguese away. For you, Mario-Bab, the Portuguese were bad; isn't that so? Why don't you condemn the Indian soldiers, now? Haven't you heard what they are doing? They drink like pigs as if they never saw drinks before; they molest and mount our women. Is that right, Mario-Bab? Only yesterday, in broad daylight, a lady teacher was raped by them at the Margão Railway Station. They loot and rape and not a single Goan opens his mouth in protest! Is this liberation, Mario-Bab?"

Agnela looked at Mario and Thomas with contempt, as if wanting to spit in their faces. "Did you ever close your doors during the Portuguese time, Ocobae?"

"No."

"In this liberated Goa, we have to stay indoors; we're prisoners in our own houses..."

"Agnela..." Thomas began, but she gave him no chance to continue. "At Bogmalo," she said, "The Indian soldiers, whom you call liberators, wanted to load themselves with free food and drink, but when the restaurant-owner refused their demands, they went into a rage! Who was this *Goawalla* to refuse them! They're the conquerors, aren't they? They came in the night and threw a hand grenade into his sleeping room, killing his daughter. You call these people liberators, do you, Mario-Bab? Do you, Thomas-Bab? In Calangute, a teacher named Germano da Sousa was killed. Who killed him? The Indian soldiers. A young boy of twelve was killed at Cansaulim. Who killed him? The Indian soldiers. At Alto-Porvorim two Hindu girls were kidnapped. Who kidnapped them? The Indian soldiers. Mario-Bab, these liberators are rampaging through Goa. Our Goa is gone!"

Some of the villagers clapped their hands at her outburst.

"You know Mario," Thomas said before leaving, "Nehru said that there would be a few inevitable casualties in a war of liberation."

CHAPTER XXXV

Contrary to some Goan fears, the Indian military administration wasn't intended to be permanent and elections were set for the 19th December 1963. The rural landlords and the commercial bourgeoisie were worried. They knew that Nehru was the only possible guarantor of their privileges, and according to the newspapers, he was some kind of a socialist or even a communist. Others noted that however often, like a fairy godfather, he waved his magic wand on behalf of the poor and landless, there had never been any significant agrarian reform. In Cavelossim, the villagers got the impression that Nehru was like senhor Tolentinho Furtado, their most revered fidalgo.

Whatever the truth about Nehru, the commercial bourgeoisie and the landed aristocracy decided that they had to act to safeguard their interests. They formed a party, the United Goans, under the leadership of Dr. Jack de Erasmo Sequiera, an aristocrat and businessman. The other party that emerged was the Maharashtrawadi Gomantak, led by Mr. Dayanand Bandolkar, who in the minds of some nonbrahmin Hindus was the reincarnation of Chattrapati Shivaji, Maharashtra's warlord, who had often made forays into Goa of yore, almost driving the Portuguese into the Indian Ocean. His party was backed by the neighbouring state of Maharashtra which had designs on annexing Goa. If Bandolkar could win the hearts of nonbrahmin Hindus, it was possible that he could win the elections.

In the election, Catholic and Hindu brahmins were on one side and nonbrahmin Hindus on the other. The Goan freedom-fighters, who mostly belonged to Nehru's Indian National Congress, had no chance of winning a single seat. In Cavelossim, which came under the Benaulim constituency, posters had gone up urging the voters that a vote for the United Goans was a vote for Goa. A vote for Maharashtrawadi Gomantak was a vote to hand over Goa to Maharashtra. Who wanted to do that? The debate went on.

After one of the political meetings in Cavellosim, Mario came up on the platform. Seeing him in a *kasti*, the outfit of the old-time Goan labourer, and holding a *pezecho-podgo* in his hand, the audience laughed. Pity the madman. If he were wise, he could reap the benefits of the sacrifices he had made in Goa's cause. Yet some were curious to hear what Mario would promise them.

For a moment, half-naked in his kasti, Mario was caught in the glow of the setting sun. Oji-mai Concentin, who was in the audience, remembered the day she had delivered him. She had never doubted that Mario was a divine child. Hut João, Tar Menin, Neunita Figueiredo and many other old-timers in the audience still believed that Mario might have something to offer them. Rosa remembered the Cross, her son's bride-in-waiting; was she still pursuing him?

"Brothers and sisters," he said when there was eventually silence. "I have news."

"What news?" a man from the audience asked.

"I have a vision of a paradise, a paradise of love."

A mixture of outright laughter and embarrassed silence greeted him, but he continued as if unaware of the derision. "In Goa, we're still united with a bond of love. When I was young, I thought love was a string and Goans were beads strung onto it, like rosary beads. We understand what virtue is and our morality isn't yet corrupt. Our duty is to strengthen the love that binds us together. If we break the string, the beads will be scattered. In the welfare of your brothers and sisters lies your own welfare. Since man can't live without food, our economic policies shouldn't deprive our brothers and sisters of their livelihood. If we do that, the cord that holds us will weaken and break and won't hold us any more. Then, liberation will be no liberation, it will be enslavement."

"What do you mean?" someone from the audience asked. "What policies are you proposing?"

"Throwing off the colonial yoke makes no difference if we don't liberate ourselves. We will step from one tyranny into another."

"If this isn't liberation, what is?" another asked.

"In each of us there are innate qualities which make us human. But often, under political and economic systems, hate and greed are planted in our souls, making us break the cord that binds us. Then we butcher our own brothers and sisters, we let our own brothers and sisters starve; this isn't liberation. True liberation is when we recognise our innate virtues and guard them from polluting influences."

The audience was becoming increasingly restive. Some were walking away from the meeting and others were talking and laughing among themselves.

"Don't think you're free and liberated just because democracy has been introduced in Goa. Far from it. Our leaders will talk honeyed words and promise heaven on earth; moneyed people will use honeyed words and promise material rewards. But they'll all have ulterior motives. In the name of religion, they'll speak against your brothers and sisters and massacre them, and call themselves holy. They'll propagandize day in and day out, brainwashing you, and call it democracy. There will be so many voices toiling to destroy your innate morality and trying to corrupt you. If they succeed, if they make you think that only money is important, they'll take your lands in the name of progress, and once your lands are gone, you won't grow your own paddy, your own vegetables, your own fruits nor raise your own poultry. You'll depend for your basic needs on others. In the name of education, you'll forsake your trades and craftsmanship. In the name of progress, the sea which once provided you with fish will be harvested by others, and you'll end up with no fish on your plate. If you allow this to happen, there'll be no joy in your soul, you'll be as good as dead. And then, you'll be thrown into a hopelessness and despair such as you've never experienced before. Let your energies, your creative forces help you to live as a single people, loving and caring for one another."

"This is all very noble, but do you want us always to be poor?" a young man from the audience asked.

"No," answered Mario. "But to be poor isn't a crime. Those who force a man into poverty are criminals and those who do not stop them are as bad."

"Why are you dressed in kasti?" the same young man asked. "Shouldn't we have done with the feudal past?"

"I don't want to see the innate virtues that the common Goan possesses being polluted by the greed of the new rich, men far more corrupt than our old landlords. We should be proud of the kasti, there's nothing degrading about it; it's better to stick to your own ways than to dream the dreams of the rich."

By this time only a handful of the crowd remained. Even for some of these, Mario was merely a curiosity, though a few were touched by what he had to say.

"Mario should have become a priest, he talks like one," said Fernando Furtado, the son of a Cavelossim notable, puffing on his cigarette. "Nothing is built on the foundation of love. Everything is built on self-interest."

"You're right," said Thomas Rodrigues. "Love and righteousness can't solve anything; they are only comforting ideas for simple minds, totally impractical. We might well be confronted by the problems created by greed and hate, but it's greed and hate in turn that will solve them, not love."

"How?"

"By giving the poor real desires, by teaching them to hate the rich. Class and caste wars, my friend! Then the poor will hate the rich for exploiting them for centuries. They'll destroy people like you, they'll destroy your caste and class. No more platitudes. Let Mario preach them to birds, like Saint Francis of Assisi!"

"You're just a dirty communist!" Fernando said, spitting on the ground.

CHAPTER XXXVI

When the first Chief Minister of liberated Goa, Dayanand Bandokar passed away in August 1973, his daughter, Mrs. Sashikala Kakodkar was crowned as president of the Maharashtrawadi Gomantak Party and Chief Minister of Goa.

She was a shrewd and tyrannical woman with a gluttonous appetite for political power. In her Council of Ministers she held sixteen portfolios, as if she were an all-round expert on Goan politics and economics; the rest she divided between two of her most trusted ministers. Mrs. Kakodkar had a shrewd knowledge of the workings of both the notables' and the peasants' minds. For instance, in Benaulim, with a Catholic majority, she chose a young Catholic and a commoner, Francisco Ferrão, to represent her party. Campaigning for Ferrão, she put before the Benaulim aristocrats, who had once hated commerce, the lure of joining the commercial bourgeoisie in the new plenty. But as the old ways were being put aside, there was an older generation of both peasants and landlords who couldn't adjust.

In Cavelossim, as in other villages, the old aristocrats, who had once been the backbone of village politics, fell silent. Many of these relics of Portuguese colonialism had died, among them Senhor Tolentinho Furtado, the father of Cavelossim village nationalism. He had passed away without any fanfare, his role in Cavelossim politics entirely forgotten. Only Tar Menin, his loyal and devoted mundcar, cried for him at Josinho's Taverna. Drunk, he delivered eulogies for his batcar and beloved leader.

There were still some old-timers left. Modo-mai Majakin, the Jaques' household laundress, was very old and bent, though she still walked the village, staff in hand. If Mario preached in Cavelossim, she would go to hear him. She would snap, "What good is liberation if we don't love each other? What good is liberation if we don't respect each other? You people say that in Portuguese times the batcar used to exploit us. Who's exploiting us now?" The young laughed at her and thought she'd gone senile.

Oji-mai Concentin was still alive, though her caste occupation wasn't in demand any more. Women now gave birth in hospital and not at home. Sometimes, she would tell of Mario's birth to her grandchildren, and they would listen to her, puzzled.

Neunita Figueiredo, Mario's godmother, wished she was dead. The old values that she cherished were no longer respected. When the lower castes called her Bae, she sensed in the inflection of their voices that they were teasing her. Suddenly, one day, she dropped dead in her house.

Hut-João, Mario's godfather, always went to listen to his godchild. He believed in him, and saw himself with his godchild in the paradise of his dreams. Plough Francis was also an ardent admirer. But when he told the young people how infant Mario had opened the doors of heaven and bought rain to a drought-stricken Goa, they would laugh at him and call him an idiot.

Tar Menin dragged himself along the village pathways. The new politics meant nothing to him, and the new politicians, he thought, were worthless. He looked forward to joining his batcar and though he knew that the old days would never return, he too went to hear Mario, because it gave him something to think about. He was there when Mario began, "Once, when I was young, my teacher Apolinario told us a fable. Do you want to hear it?"

"Yes," answered the audience.

"Once upon a time, there was a fox. This fox, whom we'll call Mr. Fox, could hardly find any food. All the coops were well guarded, as were the ducks on the pond by women with hawklike eyes. The piglings in their pens were well guarded too. Huge dogs guarded them. Mr. Fox survived by rummaging in the village garbage for anything he could find to eat. Sometimes, Mr. Fox would succeed in catching an unappetizing crawling animal for his food. He was nothing but skin and bones. But he still dreamt of feasting upon a hen for breakfast, a duck for lunch and a piglet for supper. One day, he had an idea."

"What idea?" the audience asked.

"One night," Mario continued, "Mr. Fox went to a village coop and, staying at a safe distance, he howled, 'You hens and roosters, listen to me. I have vast fields of grain. They aren't far away from your coop. Come and see them. I'll let you feed on them for nothing. What can I do with fields of grain? I don't eat grain, they're of no use to me. I know what meagre rations you're given! Come, take advantage of these vast grain fields. They're yours for nothing if only you'll risk the joys of freedom!'

"Every night Mr. Fox described these immense grain fields. Each grain, he said, was succulent and tasty. The hens and roosters, packed in the coop, couldn't resist the temptation. Even though they knew that foxes prey on fowls, Mr. Fox's expressions of concern for their welfare had blunted their instincts. They were fed up in the coop; that wasn't living. They knew their fate. Men raised them for the table. What choice did they have? They felt they could trust Mr. Fox; he seemed different.

"'If one doesn't take a chance in life, one doesn't achieve anything,' said a hen in the coop. She urged her rooster to be bold enough to verify Mr. Fox's story.

"The next night, Mr. Rooster crowed that he would come and see the vast grain fields. This made Mr. Fox very happy. At long last, he had touched the mentality of the roosters and hens in the coop. In the morning, Mr. Rooster went to meet Mr. Fox who took him to the paddy fields, and said, 'All this is yours, my friend!' Mr. Rooster had never seen such wealth of grain in his life. 'Don't be shy, my friend,' Mr Fox said. 'Go and eat as much as you want. Spread this good news to your friends. Once you have experienced this life, you'll never want to live in the coop again.'

"Mr. Rooster stepped into the paddy field and hesitantly pecked at a grain of rice. But soon, he became bold enough and started pecking hungrily. Mr. Fox knew that his days of hunger were over. Soon, he would live like a king.

"Mr. Rooster could hardly walk back to the coop, his gizzard almost touched the ground. That night, Mr Rooster addressed the other members of the coop. 'Even if we eat the grain day and night, we wouldn't finish it in our lifetime,' he said. The hens and roosters didn't doubt him. They had seen his gizzard.

"'Besides,' said Mr. Rooster, 'the grain is fresh and tasty. I never ate anything like that before. I've made up my mind. I'm leaving the coop with my hen and chicks. Those who want to come along with me are most welcome. I don't want to end up on the table, nor do I want my hen and chicks to share that fate. Come, you hens and roosters with your chicks, if you don't want to end up on the table. Let us go and claim those vast fields of grain. They are ours for nothing.'

"There was no need to persuade them further. Who would live in the coop, knowing that they were raised for the table? What a good

168 LINO LEITÃO

friend was Mr. Fox. There were hardly any animals left like that any more. Someone did point out that, by instinct, foxes are fowl eaters, but that didn't seem important any more.

"They all made up their minds that the very next day, when the coop was opened, they would sneak to freedom. At the request of Mr. Rooster, they all crowed three hurrahs to Mr. Fox, their best friend. They also crowed three hurrahs for Mr. Rooster and praised him for his daring in leading them to freedom. In their excitement, a Poet Chick composed a song which they all sang:

> 'No more coop
> No more knife
> No chicken
> In the soup
> That's the life
> What a beautiful life!'

"As soon as the next day dawned and the coop's door was opened, Mr. Rooster led the roosters, hens and chicks to freedom. All the way to the fields of grain they sang the Poet Chick's song. They were happy. They would live there, happily, ever after.

"In the same way, Mr. Fox enticed the ducks and the pigs. And when they were in his hold, Mr. Fox had a tender, fat rooster for his breakfast and succulent hens for snacks. Fat, tender ducks for his lunch and suckling piglets for his supper. For his more ostentatious banquets, which he often threw for his friends, plump hens, roosters, ducks and piglets were all featured on the menu. For days and days, his friends talked about Mr. Fox's parties.

"What's the moral?" the audience asked.

"There are many morals in this fable," Mario said. "But one that I want to point out is this: Once we ended up on the colonial table, but now, under this democracy, we are swallowed up by democratic foxes, and the tragedy is that we don't realize that we are ending up in their stomachs."

"Garbage!" remarked Menino Jesus. "His preaching won't have any impact on the masses, specially when a carrot is being dangled before their eyes!"

"Nothing has gone in your head," said Tar Menin. "You're like the fox in the fable."

"Maybe," retorted Menino Jesus, "the future of a country is entrusted to the fox and not to the parable preachers."

CHAPTER XXXVII

When Prime Minister Jawaharlal Nehru died in 1964, Lal Bahadur Shastri succeeded him, but he too was called by God within two years. The obsequious Nehruites took Shastri's death as the opportunity to consolidate their power in Congress. As interim Prime Minister they brought in Indira Gandhi, Nehru's only progeny, as a suitable figurehead to attract the piety of the masses. But as party members squabbled, she dismantled Congress and established her own party, baptising it as Congress I; the "I" standing for her name her opponents claimed. This new Empress of India then declared a state of emergency, making a mockery of the parliamentary system, and though she imprisoned contrabandists and smugglers, she also imprisoned her critics such as the saintly Vinoba Bhave. When she brought in the policy of forced sterilization, rumour had it that her son Sanjay, with his gang, went out chopping off penises. In the villages, wives slept clutching their husbands' pricks, lest Sanjay come when they had fallen asleep. Sometimes, a wife would cry out hysterically in the middle of the night, fearing that her husband's prick had gone. Finding it merely shrunken, she would give a sigh of relief. Sanjay played havoc with the sexual psyche of the people.

Opposition to the emergency was stiffer than the Empress expected, so declaring its objectives accomplished, she announced national elections. Her enemies banded together to form the Janata Party, a strange assortment of political views and hues. But Janata drove Indira out and brought the urine-drinking Moraji Desai to power.

Moraji Desai, orthodox Hindu that he was, wanted a total ban on cow-slaughter and prohibition. India's secular status was under threat, the rights of the minorities endangered. He had a vision of an orthodox Hindu India, he had no vision to free India from poverty. He was stubbornly determined to take revenge upon Indira and destroy her politically. As he was busy doing so, food prices rose, infuriating the middle class and the poor. While the new rulers were self-destructing, the dethroned Indira rose once again. The people would vote her into power again.

In Goa, the Chief Minister, Shashikala Kakodkar, had tried to emulate Indira Gandhi. Though she had tarmacked the narrow dirt roads and brought an unreliable electricity supply to the villages, Goans didn't appreciate her. Many still saw her as a traitor who wanted to hand over Goa to Maharashtra. Her own party members weren't happy with her either; she would shout at them in public, as if they were her delinquent children. As members and ministers brawled in the Goan assembly, throwing books and chairs at one another, Mrs Kakodkar did an Indira. The assembly was dissolved and President's rule was imposed. Things in the United Goans Party weren't rosy either. These upper caste Hindus and Catholics, though they had succeeded in blocking the Maharashtra merger had made little impact on Goan politics. Most of them were old pro-Salazarists, very caste-oriented and hence unable to reach out to ordinary Goans. There were splits and fallings out. Soon the United Goans weren't united any more and the majority of the United Goans joined Indian National Congress (U), not Congress I, whilst the minority went to Janata. Then new elections were called. The party leaders, candidates and their support-ers went back and forth in trucks, on the village roads, shouting their catchy slogans, soliciting support for their respective candidates and mudslinging their opponents. In this new democratic age, smugglers, criminals and even an airline hijacker got elected to the Lok Sabha in India, and in the Goan assembly things were little better.

Mario, in despair, raised his eyes to the sky and preached his vision of Paradise, but hardly anyone listened to him or took him seriously.

One evening, on the way home, Mario saw a big crowd outside Carmona. Standing at the back, he saw it was his old friend, Tomasinho Rodrigues, giving an election speech.

His voice rang out, "The first government in liberated Goa was a government of corrupt individuals. Corrupt to the very bone! Look at our businessmen and mine owners and our notables. Take a hard look at them. Weren't they the same individuals who were courting Salazar's regime before? Weren't they?"

"They were! They were!" the crowd shouted back.

"In the heydays of Salazar's regime, they licked the Portuguese officials' boots and maybe licked their arses too. These are liars and cheats, my friends. Can you solve this riddle?"

"What riddle?"

"He's short. He's bald. He's a businessman. He has money invested in trawlers. He was the friend of the Portuguese Governor, now he's the friend of the big bosses in New Delhi. He's a gambler, he's a womaniser and heavy drinker. Who is he?"

The audience shouted the name.

"No names please! I know you know him. Can you figure out this one? Tall, thin, he defected from his party and joined the other one and robbed church properties. Who is he?"

"We know him too."

"And this one? He's an M.L.A. He's a physician. He has the monopoly of bus routes and comes to the Assembly to doze. He has made the Assembly his dormitory!"

"We know him too!"

"Kunbis! Gaudis! Fisherfolks! Mar, Chamar, all outcastes, arise! Arise! Sudras, too, arise! This democracy will never make you whole! You know why?"

"Why?" asked Kunbi Jacki.

"Because India and Goa are ruled by the upper castes and moneyed classes. They're the cause of your humiliation. They treat you like dirt! Arise, my brothers, arise! Be whole persons and believe in yourselves. Unite! You're the majority! They've trampled upon you too long. Arise and drive away the beast that's been oppressing you for ages. Kill that beast, once and for all, only then will you be liberated for good!"

Mario left, shaking his head, disappointed in his old friend.

The Goan Congress U were seriously worried that Tomasinho might take the Benaulim constituency. They came up with a solution. They disposed of the former candidate who had held the constituency under the United Goans, but who was now a member of Congress U, and gave the ticket to Deus Gracias. This was a wise move for he came from a lower caste, the majority caste of the constituency, but had become the successful owner of a soda factory. Many admired him as a man who showed how the common man could make it. Though during the Emergency, he had been thrown into Fort Aguada on charges of smuggling, he was now an honest politician and his posters, complete with a saintly smile, appeared all over Benaulim. The newspapers took him into their hearts. If elected, they wrote, he would be in a position to do so much, not only for his constituents, but Goans at large.

He was shrewd. He told his constituents: "If you elect me, you won't regret it. Who knows your problems and aspirations better than I? I am one of you. If you elect me, the first thing that I'll do is to help your sons and daughters."

"How?" the audience asked.

"Your sons and daughters want to go to the Gulf, don't they? You know how difficult it is to obtain a passport, don't you? You waste a lot of money, don't you? You have to bribe and even then you don't get it. That isn't right. If you elect me, I'll make sure that you get your passports without any hassle. I'll see that you have a recruiting agency to recruit your sons and daughters to go to the Gulf. I know that you pay lots and lots of money to the agents who often run away with your money. I know your hardships. I'm your man. Vote for me!"

"We will! We will!" the audience shouted.

"If I am elected, I will open beach resorts at Benaulim, Cavelossim, Carmona and other places. More tourists will come to Goa. You'll have your own hotels and restaurants. You will be businessmen like me. Capital? Don't worry about it. I'll see that the banks give you loans. You will own your own businesses. I'll see that the tourist industry benefits you all. I'm your man. Vote for me and I'll open the doors for you. And you know what?"

"What?"

"You all know my passion for sports, don't you? When you elect me, I'll donate from my own pocket a thousand rupees to each village club. My heart cries when I see our young men loitering in the taverns. I'll take them away from the taverns and introduce them to various sports. Some great man said, 'A healthy mind in a healthy body.' I want our young men healthy in mind and healthy in body. The future of Goa should be in the hands of strong minds and healthy people. My fellow Goans, I have a lot of schemes for you. I'm your man. Vote for me!"

Tomasinho Rodrigues didn't stand a chance. When it was heard that Deus Gracias was so generous that he gave a bottle of feni to his male employees every Christmas; and gave a sewing machine to each female employee, what wouldn't he give, if elected?

And when the results came, Deus Gracias had won.

Shashikala Kakodkar's party was almost wiped out, Congress U winning a victory of landslide proportions. But since Indira's party was in power in New Delhi, what was the benefit of remaining Congress U? So a new era started in Goa: the regime of the Congress I.

CHAPTER XXXVIII

Goa marched forward. Many of the politicians who had once lived in mud houses with cow-dung floors, now had palatial mansions, chauffeur-driven cars and threw ostentatious parties. In the name of progress, all manner of evils came racing into Goa and the Goans, brought up under dictatorship and religious authority, didn't know how to handle such things.

Mario was pained. The rosary was broken and the beads were scattered. He tramped the villages preaching like a Hindu sanyasin, but he couldn't string the rosary beads together again. He was a madman, a curiosity from the past.

That summer, the sun came down like fire from Hell. There were deaths from sunstroke, and those living were parched for a drop of water. Wells, ponds and rivers ran dry. Old people remembered a summer like this before, the summer just before Mario's birth. Old memories revived and Goans flocked to the churches and chapels and took the statue of St. Anthony in procession, begging him for rain. But though the old people of Cavellosim spoke of the miracle of that earlier year, who of the younger generation could believe such fairy tales?

In the Church of the Holy Cross in Cavelossim, Rosa looked at the saints. Even she couldn't help thinking that the electric lights, installed in the church a couple of years ago, made the saints look like dolls. Gone too was the church's consecrated silence, lost in the drone of the electric fans hanging from the ceiling. Yes, Rosa recalled, the Holy Cross had given her a son, but he had given her nothing but sorrow. In the past, when the Holy Cross had come to her dreams, as a wooden bride for her son, she had feared for him. For a long time now, the Holy Cross had been absent from her dreams. Did the Holy Cross detest her son too? Who wouldn't? Who would love a madman who went about kasti-clad? What would happen to him when she died? Why hadn't Mario settled down and married?

The preacher came into the pulpit. He was not like the preachers of yore. He didn't splash his sermons with Latin phrases, nor did he pound the pulpit. This fellow's sermon didn't touch her at all.

As the congregation left the church after the service, they saw
Mario in the pavilion, kasti-clad with the pezecho podgo in his hand.
Rosa paused and looked at him, pained with love. Oji-mai Concentin
saw him too. She hadn't forgotten the rain that had ended the long
drought and she was sure that infant Mario had something to do with
it. To her, all this seemed only as yesterday. Her tongue parched with
thirst, she walked to Mario and begged, "Mario-Bab, save us all from
this drought, as you did once before."

Plough Francis, Hut João, Tar Menin and a few other old-timers,
tarried to listen to Mario preach. In this desperate hour, they had
nothing to lose.

"My brothers and sisters!" Mario began.

A hush descended and a flight of crows flew overhead, cawing.

"Listen, you poor of Goa, poor of India and poor of the world, the
rich and powerful will always keep you poor. Know their ways but do
not tread their path, for they walk the road of greed. When greed is
immense, hate is infinite. The greater the hate, the greater is the
power of destruction. Brothers and sisters, be paupers in greed but
rich in love. Your exploiters will fight among themselves and destroy
themselves. That's the way of greed. That's the way of hate. Love
alone will turn this earth into paradise."

"But Mario-Bab, I'm thirsty!" cried Pelegrina, the ten year old
granddaughter of Oji-mai Concentin. Others sighed. What had this
to do with their thirst?

"Come here, Pelegrina," Mario called.

Pelegrina, shyly, walked to Mario.

The congregation watched fretfully as Mario poured the last
drops of water that he carried in his podgo into his coconut shell.

"Dip your finger into this coconut shell and put a drop of water
on your parched tongue." said Mario.

"No, Mario-Bab," she said. "You put a drop of water on my tongue."

Mario dipped his right index finger into the coconut shell and put
a drop of water into her mouth.

"Are you still thirsty, Pelegrina?" he asked her.

"No, Mario-Bab. I'm quenched! I'm quenched!" she cried.

The congregation was still wavering. But Oji-mai Concentin called,
"Put a drop of water on my tongue and let me not die of thirst."

"Come here, Oji-mai," he said affectionately. He dipped his
finger into the coconut shell and, putting a drop of water into Oji-
mai's mouth, asked, "Are you still thirsty, Oji-mai?"

"I'm quenched! I'm quenched!" she joyfully shouted.

Tar Menin, Plough Francis, Hut João and others in that gathering came to Mario. They put their tongues out and he put a drop of water on their tongues. All felt that he had quenched their thirst.

The last to come was Apolinario, Mario's old teacher. As he dragged his feet towards him, Mario saw his teacher's brass-rimmed eyeglasses and his stoop. He looked very old and a sudden emotion squeezed Mario's heart. This was the teacher who by his own initiative had started the village school. It was here the children of the village downtrodden had learnt to read and write.

"Put a drop of water on my tongue, Mario," said Apolinario.

Mario put a drop of water on his teacher's tongue.

"I'm quenched!" said Apolinario, his face lighting up.

"Have you all quenched your thirst?" Mario asked.

"Yes!" they said.

"Look my brothers and sisters," said Mario. "All of you quenched your thirst and there's still some water left in the shell."

Plough Francis said loudly, "Ocobae's son unlocked the doors of heaven once and brought rain to our parched land. He brought hope and joy to our hearts. He'll do it again."

Mario said, "What is love? It's sharing. When you share, there's plenty. When you share, you're content, you're fulfilled. But when you grab, there's never enough. When you grab, you fight. When you grab, you hate and destroy. When I was young, it was Mestri Apolinario who taught me how to love and share."

"I?" Apolinario asked, his cheeks bathed in tears.

"Yes, my teacher, you. Despite opposition from our notables, and without any financial remuneration, you taught the children of the lower castes. You understood before anybody did in this village that all men are born equal. You're a great man, Mestri!"

"Thank you!" said Apolinario overcome with emotion.

"I must thank you; and you know why?" said Mario. "Mestri, you taught me not to put my faith in wealth or fame. You taught me to put my faith in love. In love, you are happy and free."

When Mario's preaching had come to an end, and as the congregation was dispersing, Tar Menin spoke, "Ocobae's son performed a miracle tonight. It was the miracle of water. Through it he showed us that loving, sharing and caring for each other are the only things that matter."

They went home in silence, still scanning the sky.

CHAPTER XXXIX

After the villagers had left, Mario stood looking at the Church of the Holy Cross. He remembered the struggle that had gone into making it a church, the passions that had then consumed the villagers. As the church bell rang the angelus, he recalled senhor Tolentinho Furtado, the father of Cavelossim's independence. Facing the church, he said his prayers.

He started when someone patted him on his shoulder and said, "Hi, Mario!"

Turning, he saw a young man, wearing sunglasses and dressed in a white, short-sleeved shirt.

"Yes?"

"Come," said the man, holding Mario's arm in a firm grip. He dragged him to a car, parked near the church.

"Where are you taking me?" Mario demanded.

But the man said nothing, shoving Mario into the back seat of the car and tying up his hands with a cord.

"Now, get moving," he said to the driver.

Mario's captors were the sons of Dr. Joaquim Barros, a once famous dentist from the village of Velim, whose claim to fame was that he had extracted a rotten molar from the Portuguese Governor, Bernardo Guedes. As a loyal supporter of the Portuguese regime, Barros became a target for the nationalists, and one night his surgery was broken into and vandalised. Disturbing the vandals, Barros had suffered a heart attack, fallen and cut his head. He had been found dead in the morning. In the version put out by PIDE, Barros had been sadistically tortured before being killed, and after a thorough investigation, the ubiquitous Mario Jaques had been found guilty of the murder. The Goan Portuguese dailies had carried lengthy articles describing the murder. Joaquin Barros's sons, then in their teens, had sworn to avenge their father. But then like many young Goans they had gone to work in the Gulf for an American oil company. It was message of love had been too much, and they had decided to deal with him before returning to the Gulf.

They took him at first to their father's dentistry, which had remained shut up for years. It was dark inside and Eddie Barros lit a candle. Mario was dragged in and the door locked.

"Well," said Benny, Eddie's brother, "Let us mount this anti-Christ in the dentist's chair."

They strapped Mario to the chair and gagged him.

"You fucking son of a bitch!" shouted Benny and, remembering how Mario had made his father suffer, lashed him with a spiked leather belt. "You son of a whore! You thought you could escape from our vengeance! We're the sons of Dr. Joaquim Barros, not bastards like you!"

Mario groaned as blood trickled from his mouth and head.

"That's enough, brother," said Eddy. "He's already unconscious. We can't have him dying here."

They dumped the still unconscious Mario on the back seat of the car and drove to the Baradi Hill, at Betul, where on its plateau a whitewashed chapel stands, and in front of it, a stone crucifix, erected centuries ago by shepherds. When they arrived there late at night, the hill was deserted. They knew, too, that the chaplain never slept in the chapel's dormitory, that he went home to sleep, to be with his ageing mother.

"He thinks he's some kind of Christ, so let's see how he would like to hang from the cross," Eddie said. But to ensure that there was little chance of Mario surviving this ordeal, the brothers flogged him almost to death. Then they brought a wooden cross, which they had previously hidden on the hill, into the pavilion. On it they fastened Mario in the style of Christ's Crucifixion.

"Pity we've no nails," said Benny. "Nor a crown of thorns. But... it looks almost perfect."

"Let's hoist it up now," Eddie said, and between them they hoisted up the cross, planting it in a deep hole in the centre of the pavilion, pounding in stakes at its base to secure it.

Satisfied then that Mario would either die during the night, or in the broiling sun next day, they drove away. In any case they would then be in Bombay on their way to the Gulf.

During the night, a cool breeze touched Mario's body and for a time brought him back to consciousness and pain. He writhed, cramps assailing him. He struggled to push the pain away, but failed. He fell into unconsciousness again.

He came to again with the light of the early morning and he heard the sea moaning below. Now he was almost past pain and in his mind he was transported back to his boyhood when he had watched the kasti-clad fishermen dripping with sweat, hauling in their nets, breaking with the catch. He heard the '*soi, soi*' sound the fishermen made as they hauled the net to the shore and the curses of their wives shouting obscenities and hurling fistfuls of sand at the fish-poachers. He saw himself there, a young boy, with a *kondul* in his hand, snatching fish from the catch.

Then he was in the rice paddies. They were golden yellow; it was harvest time when all was simple and beautiful. He heard loud and clear, '*Kumba re kumba! kumba re kumba!*' ringing in the dawn, and he recognised the voice of Francis Xavier, his father's paddy-hand. At harvest time, Xavier would give him a few sheaves to thrash. He heard the singing of the reapers. Wasn't that Liban's sweet voice? He heard toddy tapper Inas singing the lyrics of Blind Migel as he climbed the coconut palms with the agility of a monkey. He heard a rooster crowing, and wondered if it could be of Ermelin's. But his village was on the other side of the river. In the cashew bushes, he heard birds sing and he knew dawn was breaking. Modon, a songster bird, perched on the top of the cross, was singing thrillingly. He was moved. At his back, beyond those blue mountains, dawn was dripping as red as his blood.

He had become delirious. He saw himself like a chick in an eggshell. The shell had cracked at the top, and through that opening he glimpsed lights of different colours and hues, all intermingling. Then, he heard the sounds of a violin, and peeping through the crack, he was surprised to see a procession headed by Ubald-Bab, the village violinist. But he had died years ago of cancer. He had never heard Ubald-Bab playing violin like that before. He recognised others in the procession; they were his villagers who had died. He saw his father there.

He heard his father say, "I'm proud of you, my son!"

"Father!" Mario cried. The old animosity between them had vanished, and he was a child lifted by his father in his loving embrace.

"My son," he heard his father say. "Have you ever heard Ubald-Bab play so beautifully? He is pleased with you; we all are. He is giving his best recital in your honour, my son."

Mario thought he had never felt so happy in his life.

At the end of the welcoming legion, he saw Nirmala. He wanted to break the shell and go to her.

"Be a little patient," he heard her say. "You'll be with me soon."

The sun was coming up and Mario slipped in and out of consciousness, calmness and delirium. He saw a huge reptile. It sneered at him, fixed him with its beady eyes and hissed, "You can't close doors on me. I've penetrated deep into the hearts of men, even those who preach love and God." Mario saw the reptile vomiting huge flames which burnt up the earth like a ball of dead, dried leaves. The reptile's eyes glowed with satisfaction. "Save the world, Mario! Save the world!" it taunted him.

CHAPTER XL

It was nine in the morning and already very hot. Mario was in a stupor, coming in and out of delirium.

Three shepherd boys, Francisco Pinto, Bosteão Pinto and Rosario Fernandes came with goats to the Baradi Hill, as they always did every morning. While their goats grazed, the boys played cards. When tired of cards, one of them would come into the pulpit, which was outside on the patio and, mimicking the chaplain, would give a sermon to his congregation – the goats and his two companions.

This morning, Francisco came into the pulpit and began, "*Devachem utor, Jesus Christachem.*"

Hardly he had spoken when he shivered, looking as if he had seen a ghost.

"What's wrong?" Bosteão Pinto shouted.

Francisco stammered.

Bosteão and Rosario ran up into the pulpit and from there they saw the man strapped to the cross, blood dripping from him. Scared, they set off running to the village of Cuncolim.

Coming to the Chaplain's house, they knocked on the door, shouting and panting, "Copelão-Bab! Copelão-Bab!"

Opening the door, the chaplain asked, "Has someone broken into the chapel?"

"No, Copelão-Bab."

"What then?"

"Copelão-Bab," said Francisco Pinto, still shaking, "There's Jesus on the cross."

" Jesus? What Jesus!"

"Jesus," blurted Bosteão. "Real Jesus, on the cross. He's bleeding. A real Jesus, Copelão-Bab."

By now, the chaplain's mother had come out, hearing the commotion.

"What's going on?" she asked.

The boys told her about the Jesus on the cross, and she listened. She was a devout Catholic, and had given her only son to the priesthood. Hadn't something like this happened in Portugal, at Fatima? Why not in Goa?

"What day is it today?"

"It's Friday, mama," answered her son.

"Go and see the Crucified Christ, my son. The drought is too long. Christ might have a message for you."

The chaplain put on his cassock and black biretta and walked with the shepherd boys to the Baradi Hill. His mother came along with them, a rosary in her hands. As they walked, the news spread. Was this the omen they had been waiting for, the signal of the ending of the drought?

The pious villagers of Cuncolim, Assolna and Velim, with lit candles and enunciating their rosaries, set off for Baradi Hill. The news spread to the other side of the River Sal and the people of Cavelossim, Carmona, Orlim, Varca and some from Benaulim came in procession.

When the chaplain saw the figure on the cross his heart hammered. Though he was a priest, there were many occasions when he wasn't sure if God really existed. He thought of all his sins of the flesh, the women that he had seduced in the confessional, and he sweated, thinking about Hell. Sure enough, there was a man on the cross. There was blood dripping from his head. Yes, He was the Christ. He was Jesus. Trembling, the chaplain knelt down, folded his hands, raised his eyes to the Crucified Christ and prayed, "Christ have pity on us. We are sinners. Please save us from this drought. Bring rain, please."

His mother knelt. The shepherd boys knelt. She enunciated a rosary loudly and others responded.

Then, a young boy from Cavelossim cried out, "That isn't Christ. Christ has a beard. This one is Mario!"

The man on the cross was Mario all right, and the chaplain got up from his knees, feeling like an idiot. But to some of the people on the hill, it didn't matter if the man on the cross wasn't Christ. If it was Mario, he certainly looked very Christ-like.

By now, the older people from Cavellosim were telling anyone who would listen to them that Mario had brought rain to a drought-stricken Goa at the time of his birth. He had saved them then. He would save them now. He had the key to open the doors of heaven and bring showers of rain. Only last night, he had performed a miracle – The Miracle of Water, as Tar Menin had described it. Tar Menin was

reminding people that once, when Mario was young, he had exor-
cized him, but it had been a futile effort. He knew then, as he knew
now, that Mario was possessed by the holy spirit.

As they watched Mario on the cross, some of the crowd wondered
about his preachings. He had told them to love one another, that they
must be spiritual beings, that they must not be blinded by the
material civilisation of the dominant nations. He had wanted Goa's
and India's civilisation to be built on the foundation of love, as
Mahatma Gandhi preached and practised. Had such teachings
brought him to this fate?

"Mario's mother! Mario's mother!" someone recognising her
called out, and the crowd made way for Rosa, escorted by Oji-mai
Concentin and Modo-mai Majakin. She knew that it was her son's
wedding day. The Cross was his bride, the bride that came in her
dreams. He would consummate his marriage, today. Tears fell from
her eyes, tears of joy and sorrow.

There were some who swore that Mario called out, "Mother" when
Rosa arrived at the cross, and others who were sure that he had
already given up the ghost. There were a few who had heard him cry
out, "Mene, mene tekel upharism!" Was he cursing them? This was
not Konkani, this was not Portuguese. It was not Latin either, or
English. Later, report of these words reached Anand Kurade, a
Sanskrit scholar from Cuncolim. He recognised that they were
Sanskrit words.

When the police arrived and took Mario down from the cross he
was undoubtedly dead. "Are you people all mad to let him die like
this?" they asked.

Rosa wanted Mario to be buried in his father's grave, but the
clergy forbade his corpse's entry into the consecrated ground of the
cemetery. She was tired and she didn't fight with them. She remembered that Mario had once told her that he wanted to be cremated and
not buried. She was unhappy about this; cremation was for Hindus,
not good Catholics, but she felt that she had no choice but to grant
his wish. He was cremated the next day, which was Saturday, at the
Benaulim crematorium, built by a defrocked Catholic priest, an
educator and social worker. Despite their feelings of unease, many
of the villagers attended Mario's cremation.

The monsoon finally came, and once again, trees, grass and rice paddies were resurrected.

The following Sunday, the villagers of Cavelossim went to the Holy Cross Church and thanked the Holy Cross. Afterwards, Tar-Menin said, "Mario has twice saved us from malignant droughts. Who will save us from the politicians?"

Lino Leitão, a native of the area about which he writes, was born
in the Goan village of Varcá, in India. He studied in Portuguese
and English schools and attended the Karnataka University in
India and Concordia University in Montreal.

His other works include: *Collected Short Tales*, *Goan Tales*
and *Six Tales*. His stories have been published by *Goa Today*,
Gulab, *Gomantak Times* (Goa); *Afro-Asian Quarterly*, *Journal
of Asian Literature* (Michigan State University), *The Toronto
South Asian Review*, *Massachusetts Review*, *Pacific Quarterly*
(New Zealand), *New Canadian Review*, *Short Story International* (New York), *The Antigonish Review* and others. *The Gift
of the Holy Cross* is his first novel.